"So, what's the story ~~with~~
my mom?"

"Story?" Leah echoed and opened the dishwasher. "Apparently they're friends."

He didn't look convinced. "Friends? That's it?"

She heard his disapproval, figured it had everything to do with her father, and her protective instincts instantly kicked in. "You know, they're adults. They can do what they like. I wouldn't get upset over it if I were you," she said baldly and grinned. "You've got bigger problems to worry about."

He stilled. "I do?"

He was so close she could feel the heat emanating from him. "What problems?"

"Your mom thinks you need a wife ."

He rocked back on his heels. "A what?"

"A wife," she repeated.

"And does she have anyone in particular in mind?"

She nodded. "Yes."

He looked incredulous. "Who?"

Leah smiled, feeling ridiculously triumphant, and then strangely uncomfortable, because he looked so out of sorts. "Me."

* * *

THE CULHANES OF CEDAR RIVER:
Family lost, family found

Dear Reader,

Welcome back to Cedar River, South Dakota! And to my latest book for Harlequin Special Edition, *The Secret Between Them*. This is the fourth book in my new series, The Culhanes of Cedar River, and I'm delighted to have the opportunity to share Leah and Sean's story with you.

I love opposites-attract stories—mostly because I think in the end, it is our similarities rather than our differences that draw us toward one another when we fall in love. Which is exactly the case with artist Leah Culhane-Petrovic and reformed bad boy Sean O'Sullivan. She's nursing a broken heart and trying to rebuild her failing career, and he's holding on to a secret he won't share with anyone. Until he meets Leah.

She discovers it takes only one person to believe in you to make you reach for the stars, and he learns that vulnerability isn't a weakness. And of course, in true romantic style, they get a little nudge along the way from Leah's widowed dad and Sean's recently divorced mom—who also happen to be in the middle of their own little happily-ever-after!

I hope you enjoy Leah and Sean's story and invite you back to South Dakota for my next book in The Culhanes of Cedar River series, coming soon. I love hearing from readers and can be contacted at helenlaceyauthor@gmail.com or via my website at helenlacey.com or Facebook page to talk about horses, cowboys or how wonderful it is writing for Harlequin Special Edition. Happy reading!

Warmest wishes,

Helen Lacey

The Secret
Between Them

———

HELEN LACEY

HARLEQUIN
SPECIAL
EDITION

Recycling programs
for this product may
not exist in your area.

ISBN-13: 978-1-335-89462-5

The Secret Between Them

Copyright © 2020 by Helen Lacey

This edition published by arrangement with Harlequin Books S.A.

For questions and comments about the quality of this book,
please contact us at CustomerService@Harlequin.com.

Harlequin Enterprises ULC
22 Adelaide St. West, 40th Floor
Toronto, Ontario M5H 4E3, Canada
www.Harlequin.com

Printed in U.S.A.

Helen Lacey grew up reading *Black Beauty* and *Little House on the Prairie*. These childhood classics inspired her to write her first book when she was seven, a story about a girl and her horse. She loves writing for Harlequin Special Edition, where she can create strong heroes with soft hearts and heroines with gumption who get their happily-ever-afters. For more about Helen, visit her website, helenlacey.com.

Books by Helen Lacey

Harlequin Special Edition

The Culhanes of Cedar River

The Nanny's Family Wish
The Soldier's Secret Son
When You Least Expect It

The Cedar River Cowboys

The Cowgirl's Forever Family
Married to the Mom-to-Be
The Rancher's Unexpected Family
A Kiss, a Dance & a Diamond
The Secret Son's Homecoming

The Fortunes of Texas: The Lost Fortunes

Her Secret Texas Valentine

The Fortunes of Texas

A Fortunes of Texas Christmas

Visit the Author Profile page
at Harlequin.com for more titles.

For my agent, Scott Eagan—
Thank you for your continuing support.
And for sometimes having to talk me down
off the ledge.

Chapter One

Sean O'Sullivan knew exactly who owned the big yellow dog that had decided to lay directly in front of his door.

Leah Culhane-Petrovic.

The most annoying woman he'd *never* met.

Her father, Ivan, lived next door, and she'd moved in with old man two days ago. He'd seen her high school graduation picture sitting proudly on the mantel above Ivan's fireplace.

She'd moved in to help care for her father, who'd had a stroke five weeks earlier. The news was obviously good for Ivan, but bad for him. Because since six o'clock the previous morning, there had been three moving vans barreling down their shared driveway, kicking up clouds of dust and gravel in their wake. The fact her two dogs had already found their way into his yard and dug holes all over the place was bad enough, but the fact that one of the yellow monsters had decided to sleep on his porch and chew the leg off a cane chair was the last straw.

He checked his watch, saw it was eleven o'clock and decided to walk over and give her a piece of his mind. It wasn't that he cared about sharing the driveway with his neighbors—he liked Ivan well enough—but Sean had moved to the house by the river for solitude, and that was all about to change. Leah was an artist and would be setting up a studio in the large shed at the rear of Ivan's yard…right near the hedge that separated the two properties. Which was where the moving vans had unloaded pallets of gear and equipment the previous day.

There goes my privacy.

The more he thought about it, the more irritated he became. Enough to grab his jacket, shove his feet into boots, pick up the house keys and head through the front door. The dog followed him down the path and through the hedge and over the worn track. The mutt started barking the moment they reached Ivan's yard and its cohort, a bigger and shaggier version, began doing the same thing, and then started racing around Sean as he made his way toward Ivan's house.

It wasn't that Sean didn't like dogs—he'd had one or two as a kid—he just didn't like the idea of someone else's lounging on his porch. Because it smacked of a familiarity he was trying to avoid. And Sean had returned to his hometown of Cedar River, South Dakota, to be left alone.

If only he could get that through to his family.

It was bad enough he had to endure their well-meaning attempts to butt into in his life every few days or so, but disruptive neighbors he could do without. True, Sean had become friendly with Ivan since he'd moved into the house, and he genuinely liked the older man. Ivan was quiet, studious and didn't say much, which suited Sean just fine. The sixty-nine-year-old had no major side effects other than his slightly uneven gait, and he often used a cane to support himself. Sean sensed the former high school history teacher liked his life quiet and uncomplicated, surrounded by his books and the watercolors he painted. And Sean was happy with the mostly silent chess games—it meant he didn't have to offer any explanations for his own behavioral tics.

He climbed the steps and tapped on the door, flicking a glance sideways to the table and chairs on the wide veranda. The chess game they'd left two days ago was sitting untouched on the table. The truth was, Sean wasn't much of a chess player, but he liked that he could sit without having to talk. He could just simply concentrate on the game and purge everything else in life right out of his mind.

He waited, then tapped again. And again.

Sean heard something. He wasn't sure what. Which wasn't unusual because he was becoming increasingly used to mishearing, or simply *not* hearing things. Since the diagnosis twelve months ago, his whole life had changed. Thinking about it invoked a familiar helplessness and resentment, and he quickly pushed the feelings aside.

With no answer, he turned around to leave and then stumbled back on his heels.

A woman stood at the bottom of the steps. Recognition flickered for a moment in his mind, then quickly faded. She wore jeans and a checked shirt, a long sheepskin vest that came to her knees, mid-heeled cowboy boots and a bright orange hat. She had long, ink-black, wavy hair that hung down her back and deep green eyes. He stared at her, oddly fascinated by her riveting colors. She wasn't like the women he was usually attracted to—but somehow, she was impossible to ignore. For one, she had the most incredible hair he'd ever seen, and the more he looked the more he noticed that there were colors of pink and purple subtly threaded throughout the long waves cascading down her back. And her emerald eyes were glaring at him, filled with a mix of curiosity and suspicion. A strange sensation hit him in his gut, one he didn't want to acknowledge. Because feeling *anything* was out of the question.

Sean quickly pulled himself together and spoke. "Can I help you?" he asked.

She propped her hands on her hips and tilted her head a little. "I was about to ask you the same question."

"I was looking for Ivan."

"He's resting," she said, head still at an angle. "You must the neighbor I've heard so much about."

Again, recognition wavered inside his head, but Sean was certain he'd never met her. "You have?"

"Dad says you suck at chess."

Dad?

Sean stared at her. *This* was Ivan's daughter? Impossible. The girl in the photograph on the mantel had glasses, braces and a shy, awkward smile— definitely not the confidence of this...*woman*. He took a few steps toward the edge of the porch. "You're not his daughter... Leah."

Her shoulders tightened. "I'm not?"

Heat crawled up his neck, and he hated the fact she was making him uncomfortable. Sean didn't do *uncomfortable*. Women didn't make him tongue-tied. Women flirted with him and then usually, if things went well, fell into his bed. "You're...the picture... the one on the mantel..."

She threw her head back and laughed, exposing a long throat that hitched his awareness of her up a couple of notches. He quickly pushed the notion aside.

"Dad's favorite," she said, her green eyes wide with amusement. "He still likes to think of me as his little girl."

Sean did his best to ignore the way his heart was beating faster than usual. Perhaps because he hadn't been close to an attractive woman in months. *Not* that he thought she was attractive. He didn't go for artsy types. In the past he'd dated models and actresses who were uncomplicated and self-centered and no more interested in anything long-term or serious than he was. At the moment he didn't date anyone. Hell, he tried not to even see anyone. Just like he wanted.

He uncharacteristically tugged at his collar and hated the way her gaze followed his every move. It felt like she was watching him—examining him. And he didn't like it. All he wanted to do was bail and head home. But a good dose of ego made him stay exactly where he was and stare at her in return. Which, he realized, wasn't exactly a hardship. Sure, she wasn't his type, but he had to admit she was attractive in her own way. And he had time to kill. Since returning to Cedar River he had plenty of time.

The truth was, he'd spent the past couple of months trying to figure out what he was going to do next. He might have bailed on his career, but life still went on. Or so he'd been told by doctors and specialists. And he knew his family would say the same thing—if he told them the real reason he'd come home. He almost wished he *had* to work. But he had more money in the bank than he could ever spend and no inclination to earn more doing something he had little interest in.

"So, Dad's resting…like I said."

Her voice again, dragging him back into the moment. Sean managed a slight shrug and tried to appear indifferent either way. "Sure… I'll come back later."

She took a couple of steps forward. "You can wait for a while if you like. He usually only naps for an hour at a time. I've just made some hot chocolate."

Chocolate? Why not? It wasn't as though he had anywhere else he needed to be. And it was getting cool. Colder temperatures were forecast for later in the week, but it was a typical fall day, with enough bite in the air to require a coat and good boots. Fortunately he had both. "Ah…sure."

She smiled and her green eyes darkened. "Be back in a minute," she said as she moved up the stairs and disappeared into the house.

Sean lingered by the steps, ignoring the dogs, which were winding around his legs in turn begging for attention. They got bored with his lack of response and plopped into their beds, situated at the end of the veranda.

She returned a few minutes later, carrying a tray, maneuvering through the doorway with smooth dexterity. Her hair swayed as she walked, and he caught a glimpse of the colors hidden beneath the strands. It suited her, he thought. And something niggled at him, a kind of hazy awareness that made him shake his head. This was so ridiculous. He didn't know her. They'd never met.

"Here we go," she said, her voice almost floating on the air between them. "Please, sit down."

Sean remained where he was, watching as she

dropped a dollop of whipped cream into each mug. It both irked and amused him that she hadn't asked how he liked his drink, just assumed he'd take it the way she was offering.

He moved across the veranda and sat down, perched uncomfortably on the edge of the wicker love seat. She sat down opposite and passed him a mug. But she didn't speak. Instead, she touched the rim of her mug with her thumb and wiped away some milky foam and then popped her thumb in her mouth. The action shouldn't have registered as anything to him. But he experienced an odd feeling in the pit of his stomach. The awareness was back, only this time it didn't dissipate so easily. Sean looked at her, trying to find flaws as a way of dispelling the awareness. But it was difficult, if not impossible. Her emerald eyes especially—they were damned near perfect. And her lashes were the longest he'd ever seen; he could tell she wasn't wearing a shred of mascara.

"Dad said you were retired?"

Sean stared at her mouth. "On hiatus," he replied, ignoring the heat from the mug in his hand.

"You work in the music business?"

He shrugged. "I did."

"And movies, too?" she asked.

Sean nodded. "That's right."

Her head angled to the side a fraction. "And now you don't do anything?"

There was enough tone in her voice to sound like

criticism, and he scowled. "I'm taking a break from the industry."

"You mean taking a break from life?" she asked bluntly, pulling no punches.

Irritation wove up his spine, and he decided he didn't like this woman one little bit. "Not that it's any of your business, but I came back to Cedar River to spend time with my family."

Her brows rose dramatically. "Really? Dad said you spend most of your time alone. Unless you're here letting him beat you at chess."

His irritability increased. "My parents got divorced. My dad remarried," Sean said as an answer, and then almost jumped out of the chair the moment the words left his mouth, because he had no idea why he would say such a thing to a stranger. He certainly didn't want her knowing anything about his personal life. Not that his parents' divorce was a secret around town. But the reason they parted was still a sore issue for him.

Jonah. His half brother. Barely three months younger than he was. The son his father had kept secret for nearly thirty years, the result of an affair he'd had before Sean was born. But it wasn't a secret anymore. And now his parents were divorced and his father was married to Jonah's mother, Kathleen. His family had imploded, and it felt as though he was the only one who gave a damn, since Liam, Kieran *and* Jonah had all gotten married over the past few years and were all busy with their new families.

"I know your mom," she said, dragging his attention back into the moment and smiled, exposing perfectly even teeth. "She's been talking to me about showcasing some of my work at the art gallery in town. Your sister-in-law is the curator there, correct?"

Was there anything about his family that she didn't know?

Sean's mouth compressed into a tight line. Yes, Kayla was the gallery and museum curator *and* his eldest brother Liam's wife. "That's right."

"I'm also doing a piece for the foyer at the hotel, so I've met Liam several times."

Hmm. She was way too familiar with his family. Well, he knew some things about her, too. "You're a sculptor?"

She nodded. "Yes. I work mostly with metal. But I also paint a little, and do pottery."

"A triple threat."

She grinned. "Thank you. So, what's with the mountain man look?" she asked, still smiling.

Sean frowned and rubbed a hand over his jaw and the two-month-old beard growth, and then had the irritated thought that what the hell difference did it make, anyway, if he chose not to get a haircut or shave. "Are you the barber police?"

"Are you always such an unbearable grouch?"

Then she laughed. *At him*. He felt it through to his bones. And Sean wasn't used to being laughed at.

He placed the mug on the table and got to his feet. "I have to get going. Thanks for the chat and the cocoa."

"Anytime… Sean."

He ignored her, then walked across the veranda and headed down the steps, striding toward the hedge and away from the most annoying woman he'd ever met. One he hoped he'd never meet again, even if that meant *not* catching up with Ivan.

Minutes later he wiped his boots on the mat on his porch. As he slammed the door to the house, a thought registered in his brain and he groaned. He'd been so eager to get away from her, he hadn't mentioned anything about the damned dog!

It was a universally known fact that Leah Culhane-Petrovic had poor taste in men. The very worst taste, in fact, according to her brother, David, or any one of her cousins who lived in town. The last bad choice had swindled her out of a sizable chunk of her savings and stolen several pieces of her best work. The police hadn't been much help trying to recover the art, and by the time they'd caught up with her ex, he'd lost most of her cash at the craps tables in Vegas. It was a valuable lesson learned. *Trust no one.* Particularly not uber good-looking men who oozed charm and sexiness and showed interest in a woman who was average looking at best and clearly didn't know how to make good choices.

Of course, Xavier hadn't been the first jerk to cross her path. That was Gary Billings, *art dealer to the stars*, who turned out to be *married Gary*, and about the worst art dealer on the West Coast. He hadn't managed to sell a single piece of her work after nearly eighteen months. True, he didn't steal anything, but he did lie his ass off the entire time they were together.

So, at twenty-seven, she'd sworn off *all* men and decided to look after the one who'd never let her down—her father, Ivan. And now that he was slowly returning to good health, she could begin to concentrate on her career again. In the past year, well before Ivan's stroke, she'd sold several small pieces and had orders for two more, including one for the foyer of the O'Sullivan Hotel in the middle of town. The same hotel owned by Sean O'Sullivan's family.

Even with his shaggy hair and unshaven jaw, he was to-die-for sexy. He still had the same broad shoulders and loose-limbed frame. And he was still the same guy who'd ignored her completely the last time their paths had crossed. Admittedly, it had been eight years ago, but for her the memory was still there. She'd been back for the Christmas break from college in Denver, visiting her parents, and had brought along her roommate who'd been alone for the holidays because her family was in Europe on vacation. They'd made their way to the bar at the O'Sullivan Hotel for a few laughs and a pitcher of sangria, and he'd walked in with one of his brothers and a couple of friends. She'd heard he'd moved to

Los Angeles a few years earlier, but returned a couple of times a year to visit his family.

Back then she'd had a serious crush on him, naively ignoring his wild reputation with women. Not that he'd ever look in *her* direction. No, rumor had it that Sean O'Sullivan had a type. Tall and thin and blond. Like her friend Carissa—who ended up spending the weekend with him at the hotel. When he'd said hello to Leah at the bar, she had been flattered and hopeful, but quickly realized he was only interested in her tall, willowy friend. Of course, he hadn't lasted with Carissa. He returned to California three days after that, and Carissa saw him in LA a few weeks later, before the relationship fizzled. She'd lost touch with her friend after college, and the last Leah knew, Carissa had married an investment banker and lived in Texas. It proved to Leah that Sean O'Sullivan was a womanizing jerk.

The years seemed to have changed him, though— he didn't appear to be the arrogant, commitment phobic playboy who had a different woman in his bed every weekend, because according to her father, he'd rarely ventured out in the evenings since he'd bought the house by the river. Not that Leah had listened to her father's conversations about his new neighbor with a whole lot of interest. Her fleeting infatuation with Sean O'Sullivan had ended years ago. Still, it irked her that, first, he didn't recognize her from the picture on the mantel, and second, that she was so forgettable, period.

He's still shallow and always will be.

"Who is?"

Leah turned from her task of preparing lunch, realizing she had said the words out loud. Her father came into the kitchen, his walking stick clicking on the linoleum, followed by the familiar sound of his shoe scuffing over the floor as his left leg dragged slightly behind him. Ivan Petrovic had a short, trimmed gray beard, glasses and a shiny bald head. Her mother, Sandra, had died five years earlier in a plane crash. Leah had a half brother, David McCall, who was an accountant and lived on his family's small ranch outside of town with his fiancée and two kids. David's first wife, Jayne, an accomplished pilot, had been flying the plane that had crashed, killing both herself and Leah and David's mother on impact.

Leah had grown up in Cedar River until she left for college when she was eighteen. After graduation, she'd made her home base in Aspen and had mostly been happy there, returning to South Dakota for the holidays. But her failed relationship with Xavier had reinforced her desire to move back home to be with closer to family, and for the last year she'd been working at a gallery in Rapid City and teaching an art class at a local technical college. However, when her father had a stroke over a month earlier, Leah knew it was time to come home for good. She wanted to help her dad with his recovery, and suggested she move in with him for a while. It took some convincing—Ivan was proud and independent and didn't like admitting he needed help. But eventually he agreed, and when he offered her the chance to turn the old shed into a studio, she jumped at the opportunity.

She pushed out a smile and shook her head. "No one, Dad," she said, answering his question. "I've made lunch."

He gave her one of his lopsided smiles. "Did I hear voices earlier?"

Her back stiffened. "Your neighbor stopped by."

"Ah… Sean. You didn't invite him to stay for lunch?" he asked, motioning to the pile of sandwiches on the plate she now carried.

Leah shrugged and placed the plate on the round oak table. "He didn't seem inclined to hang around."

Ivan nodded and sighed. "He's troubled, that boy."

"He's hardly a boy, Dad," she said and felt heat creep up her neck. She then silently called herself all kinds of stupid for letting Sean O'Sullivan garner any kind of reaction. "I mean…it's none of our business."

"Gwen's worried, I know that much."

Gwen O'Sullivan was Sean's mother. Leah raised both brows. "I didn't realize you were so well acquainted with the O'Sullivans."

She could have sworn her father's cheeks tinged with a little color and she had the fleeting thought that maybe his acquaintance with Gwen was more than a simple *acquaintance.* She'd often asked her dad why he hadn't dated since her mom died, and he'd always dismissed her questions with a wave and the insistence that he was happy alone—but she wasn't sure she completely believed him.

"We attend the same book club," Ivan said and sat down. "She's stopped by a few times since I got out of hospital. She's a nice woman."

"I know," Leah said and grinned cheekily. "And very attractive."

Her dad's brows furrowed. "Don't be reading anything into it."

"I think it's great," she said and offered another impish grin she hoped would make him smile. "About time you got a girlfriend."

Ivan's cheeks were now beet red. "It's nothing like that. We're friends."

"That's how it starts. At least that's what I've heard. Not that I'm an expert in the romance department," she said and sighed. "Not with my track record."

Her father took a sandwich from the plate and met her gaze. "There's someone special out there for you, honey. Someone who will appreciate how talented and amazing you are."

Someone who likes creativity, color and a flat chest.

"Men think I'm weird," she said and laughed.

"Well, maybe you are," her father said and smiled broadly. "Nothing wrong with being a little different."

Different? She'd been called that before. And kooky and arty and sometimes just plain old nuts. Xavier had said so many times. True, sometimes she got lost in her work and would spend days in the studio, wrapped up in the creative process, unaware of anything other than the textures of the materials and the shapes that seemed to morph through her heart and hands into something that told a story in every line and edge and arc. She couldn't explain it, and when the mood came, she didn't possess the ability to do anything other than go where inspiration took her. So if that made her weird…well, she'd own it.

"It's a nice idea, but I'm not in the market for a relationship at the moment," she said and took a bite of a sandwich. "I have to concentrate on you and getting two new pieces finished by the end of next month."

Ivan nodded. "I'm very proud of you, you know. Pursuing dreams can be hard sometimes. Your talent and commitment are really inspiring."

"You've always been my number one fan, Dad," she said and laughed. "Well, you and David, and you both might be a little biased."

"Nonsense," he scoffed. "And one day the rest of the world will know it, too."

"I'm not aiming for the world," she said soberly. "Just the odd gallery or two."

"Perhaps it's time you considered having a show again?"

Leah shook her head. She'd had a show once… and it had been a disaster. Only a handful of people had attended, and not one piece had sold. It was a humiliation she wasn't keen to repeat in a hurry. "Not yet. One piece at a time is all I'm ready for."

"Well, I know Gwen asked you to showcase a few pieces at the art gallery in town. That would be a good start."

"Yes," she said and smiled warmly. "Maybe."

She was still thinking about her father's words a couple of hours later. The shed would make a fine studio once she tidied the place up a bit. As she walked around the drafty building, she made plans for where everything would eventually go and which spots had the best light and shade. All of her equipment had arrived safely, and one side of the shed was stacked with materials and tools. There was a small room that she would turn into an office, and a loft for storage.

Once she was done, she locked up and walked the perimeter, noticing a couple of places that needed the planking repaired. Her father had suggested a local carpenter who would be able to do the work, and she made a mental note to call him the next day.

Leah called to her dogs, Betty and Wilma, and continued her walk around the building. The hedge behind it was thick and unkempt, and she spotted an area with an opening and a footpath, which led to the river and to the big log cabin that sat overlooking the water. Sean O'Sullivan's house. They shared a driveway and a mailbox. The split-log western red cedar cabin had been empty for almost a year before *he'd* moved in a couple of months ago. Leah adored the cabin, and had always longed to buy the place herself because it had the most incredible stone fireplace in the main living room and a glorious view of the river from the wide porch and would be the perfect place to sketch. There was a small paddock and stable, a boat ramp and a boathouse she often thought would make a fine studio. But it wasn't to be. Xavier had cleaned out her account, and it would take her five years—probably way more, given how slow her work was selling—to save for a deposit. And of course there was the annoying fact that O'Sullivan had snuck in like a rat up a drainpipe and stolen her dream house.

Damn Sean O'Sullivan.

As she trudged back toward the house, Leah decided she never wanted to see him again. He could find someone else's father to play chess with. Someone else's porch to linger on. As far as she was concerned, the Culhane-Petrovic property was an O'Sullivan-free zone.

And the quicker he figured that out, the better!

Chapter Two

The O'Sullivan Hotel was easily the best in several counties. With thirty-odd rooms, two restaurants, conference rooms…it was a destination stop for tourists and locals. And Sean had to admit his eldest brother, Liam, did a great job running the place. Their father, J.D., had retired several years earlier, happy to spend his time fly-fishing and perfecting his golf swing. Since the divorce, however, he was pretty sure his dad was keener to pursue his relationship, and now marriage, to Kathleen Rickard. His half brother Jonah's *mother*.

Nearly three years after discovering he had another brother, it still irked him.

Not that he *blamed* Jonah. But the whole situation

had become like a daytime soap opera. And he'd had enough drama back in LA to last him a lifetime. He just wanted a quiet, simple life so he could regroup and figure out what he was going to do with himself for the next forty or fifty years.

Sean spotted his brother at the concierge desk and strode across the foyer. Liam was the picture-perfect executive in his suit and tie. He'd been born to take over the family business once he'd finished college. Kieran had gone to medical school, and Sean had taken off to Hollywood. And their sister, Liz, had stayed in Cedar River and married a local rancher, living happily with her family until she'd passed away over seven years ago. Her husband had since remarried, but still ensured that Liz's three young daughters spent time with the family.

"You're late," Liam said as he approached.

Sean didn't bother to check his watch. "Yeah... sorry."

Liam shook his head. "It's getting to be a habit of yours. Can you at least pretend to be interested in this? I don't expect you to—"

His brother's voice faded as he turned toward the desk to grab his phone, and Sean stepped a little closer, trying to hear the other man's words. "I am," he said as earnestly as he could.

This, was to help arrange a surprise sixty-fifth birthday party for their father.

Liam turned back around. "Are you? You're so

disengaged it's hard to know what's going on in your head these days."

Self-pity.

Sean ignored the way the words smashed around him. He didn't want to be *that guy*, the one who couldn't deal with the pile of crap that had come to define his life. He'd lived the last ten years exactly as he'd wanted to, finding success in his chosen career, making more money than he could ever spend, dating too many women to remember. Now, Sean experienced an acute sense of regret. Fast cars, fast women, fast friends who came and went with the tide... Now that he was back in Cedar River, none of it seemed to matter.

"Nothing's going on," he said to his brother, and slapped Liam affectionately on the shoulder. "Where's Kieran?"

Liam hooked a thumb in the direction of the elevators. "In my office, waiting for you."

Sean shrugged and followed Liam to the third floor. When they reached the office, he spotted the hotel's assistant manager, Connie, walking from the office. Connie was also married to Jonah, and for the life of him Sean couldn't understand why such a sweet woman like Connie would fall for a guy as moody as his half brother. Jonah had moved from Portland a couple of years earlier and worked in Rapid City for one of the city's largest architectural firms. He and Connie lived halfway between both towns for an easy commute. They were also expecting their first child in a couple of months.

"Hey, Sean," she said as he passed her, and then heard her say something else he couldn't quite make out.

He stopped midstride and met her gaze. "Sorry?"

"I said, it's good to see you?"

Sean nodded. "Yeah…likewise."

She smiled and was about to say something else when Kieran popped his head around the doorway leading to Liam's private office. "There you are. Hurry up, will you? I have to get home to look after the boys while Nic works tonight."

Nicola was Kieran's wife and owned JoJo's Pizza Parlor. The boys were her two nephews, and she'd had custody of them since their parents had been killed five years earlier.

Sean now glanced at his watch. Damn, it wasn't as though he was *that* late. It was ten after four, and his presence had been requested for four o'clock. "I'm here, as I said I would be."

He walked into the office and spotted Jonah sitting on the couch against one wall, head bent and his concentration focused on the tablet in his hand. He looked up, raised a brow and then returned his attention to his electronic device. Sean wandered over to the window and stared out at the street. Cedar River was a typical small town—wide sidewalks, a mix of old and new storefronts, one set of traffic lights. At eighteen, he couldn't wait to get out of the place and head to California. He'd endured two semesters at UCLA before deciding that school wasn't his thing and then pounded the pavement, visiting every recording studio in town. He lucked into a small, barely solvent company and worked fourteen-hour days to learn the business, and a year later he spent every dime he had, plus a sizable loan from his father, to buy out 51 percent of the studio. He started producing music for a few edgy, independent bands, finding a niche working with alternative-style musicians. When one hit the more mainstream airwaves, Sean found himself producing for some of the biggest names in the business. In another two years he was doing short films. Then came awards and accolades, and he was at the top of the game by the time he was twenty-six. Life cruised along for a few years. He owned a home in Laurel Canyon, a Ferrari, his investment portfolio increased, his bank balance bulged and he knew he had it all.

Until his world turned upside down.

Irreversible sensorineural hearing loss. Progressive and incurable, caused by years of exposure to the music he'd loved all his life. He went to several specialists, and the results were always the same. Of course, he could have worked around it, relied on hearing aids for support, changed things in the studio to help himself acclimate…but he didn't *want* to make those changes. And he damn well didn't want pity. Once people knew of his condition, he'd get it, for sure. The risk of losing work, of people question-

ing his skills because of his hearing loss, quickly became a very real fear.

He hated the way he felt. Hated the pride that suddenly seemed to define him. Hated feeling as though
he would be...judged. And he was ashamed, too. Because a less proud man would have been able to deal
with the questions. And would have stayed, would
have adapted to the sounds he'd already lost, the ones
he'd always taken for granted. Like the *whoosh* of the
wind when he drove down the coast with the window
down, the intimacy of a whisper, the patter of soft
rain on the roof, a quiet conversation in a crowded
room. And those he knew he would likely lose in
the future—the music he loved, the roar of a engine
motor, the bark of a neighborhood dog... Another
man would have learned to live with the diagnosis
and adapt, not bail like Sean had...on his career and
his life, returning to the place he'd been so eager to
get away from so many years earlier.

"Did you hear what I said?"

Liam's voice echoed in his ears as his brother sidled up beside him. Sean shrugged. "Sorry, I was
miles away."

Liam frowned. "Seems that happens a lot these
days."

Sean ignored the words and took a few steps, settling on the chair near the window. Kieran moved up
next to him and sat down, and Liam spent the next
ten minutes talking about the party ceremony and
how he expected each of them to say a few words

about their father. Kieran, who was one of the most easygoing, likable people on the planet, agreed immediately and Jonah followed suit straight after.

"So...are you in?" Liam asked.

He shrugged. "Sure."

His eldest brother nodded, looked briefly at the other two men in the room and then walked toward the small bar. A minute later they all had a beer in their hands, and Sean sensed a sudden shift in the mood. The door was closed, and he was alone with his three siblings. They were all watching him, he realized. And Kieran looked particularly serious.

"Is this an intervention?" he asked, one brow cocked.

Kieran spoke next. "We're concerned about you. You're not yourself."

"Is that your medical opinion?"

Kieran sighed heavily. "It's my opinion as your older brother."

Sean sat forward in the chair, straining to hear his brother's voice. "I'm fine."

"You're not fine," Kieran said quickly. "You've come back home without an explanation, and you've holed yourself up in that big house like a hermit."

"A hermit?" he scoffed, annoyance curling up his spine. "Hardly. I'm here now."

"You're here because I wouldn't take no for an answer," Liam said, and raised both hands. "What happened to you, Sean? You're not talking and frankly, you look like hell. So, yeah, we're worried. And so are Mom and Dad. What is it? Did your business go bust? Or did you go through a rough breakup?"

Sean got to his feet and shook his head. "I *sold* my very successful business for a wad of cash, and we all know that I don't do relationships. I just wanted to come home for a while, and I don't want to get the third degree about it."

"And that's all we get? Some vague response about wanting to come home?"

He rolled his eyes. Some days he wished he was an only child. "Yes."

"I'm not buying it," Liam said. "You don't do *home*. You're a city boy, Sean. This lumberjack look and a log cabin on the lake are just not you."

Sean laughed out loud. What was with everyone's sudden fascination with his hair and his homecoming? It was ridiculous that they believed he'd come back because his business had gone bad—far from it. He'd sold the studio for an absurdly profitable amount and stopped answering his phone or checking emails because he kept getting offers to work with some big star or another. As for the other thing—to imagine he'd come back to nurse some kind of broken heart. Ridiculous. He'd never been overly invested in any relationship he'd been in— most were fleeting at best.

"It's the new me," he said and ran a hand over his bearded jaw. Kieran and Liam didn't look convinced, but he was all out of explanations. He just wanted everyone to mind their own damned business. He glanced toward Jonah and noticed that his younger brother was sitting back on the couch, arms crossed. "So, do you have an opinion too?"

Jonah shrugged one shoulder. "I don't think it would matter if I did."

"You're right about that," Sean replied. "Now, if we're done here, I have to get going. There's somewhere I have to be."

"Good," Liam said, clearly exasperated. "I hope it's a date. Might improve your mood."

Sean wasn't about to admit that he hadn't been on a date, much less had a woman in his bed, for over six months. The less they knew the better. He placed the untouched beer on Liam's desk. "See you later."

"You can't avoid us forever, Sean," Kieran said.

"Want to bet?"

He turned and strode from the office, giving a half-hearted wave to Connie and headed downstairs. He was halfway across the foyer when he spotted a familiar woman standing in the lobby.

Leah.

Someone he'd managed to avoid for three days. Like his day couldn't get any worse. She held a notepad in one hand and a tape measure in the other, and appeared to be measuring out space by the front window. He recalled she'd said she was doing an art piece for the hotel and figured it had something to do with that. He was about to ignore her and walk through the door when he noticed that his three brothers had followed him downstairs and were standing by the concierge desk.

He wouldn't be surprised if one or all of them tailed his car when he left. And his growing irritation at being watched like a hawk amplified the more he thought about it. He simply wanted to be left alone. He didn't want to deal with explanations about his life. He knew his family would suffocate him with their combined need to help him. And he didn't want help. He'd always done things his own way. Sure, he was an O'Sullivan, but he'd never used the family name or wealth to get what he wanted. He appreciated the ambition his father had driven into him when he was young, but he'd been determined to *not* ride along on the back of that wealth to make a success of his own life. Even the loan he'd accepted from his father to first purchase the studio had been paid back in full and with interest. He'd always wanted his own legacy...proof that he wasn't defined by the name he'd inherited.

But they still believed they could smother him in a blanket of O'Sullivan kindness and consideration. He wasn't ready for that. Not yet. And he doubted he ever would be. He wasn't as bound to his birthright as Liam, or as generous and compassionate in nature as Kieran. In fact, the only one who might understand his need to be left alone was Jonah, and he had no intention of spilling his guts to his younger sibling, since a part of him resented the fact that Jo-

nah's very existence was the reason his parents were
now divorced.

Before he could stop his legs from moving, he
was across the foyer and standing a foot away from
the most annoying woman on the planet. She wore a
knee-length dress, dark in color and made from some
sort of stretchy fabric. Teamed with red high-heeled
cowboy boots and a fleece-lined denim jacket, it was
a look that suited her. He'd worked with creative people for years and admired anyone who pursued their
passion. And he noticed several people were looking
at her as they passed. She turned as though sensing
someone behind her and didn't hide the surprise in
her expression.

"Oh...hello."

He watched her mouth. Her bottom lip was a little fuller than the top, and it was quite alluring. The
vivid green of her eyes made a riveting combination
with the dark lashes and steeply arched brows. And
her hair was incredible. Yeah, Leah was definitely
attractive in her own way. Not the kind of preened
and cosmetically enhanced beauty he'd become used
to over the past decade, but in a colorful and striking kind of way.

He spoke quickly, aware that his brothers were
watching him. "I need a favor."

Her brows came together. "A favor?"

"Yeah," he said, briefly glancing toward his brothers. "I'll buy you a drink."

Her generous mouth curled. "Really?"

Sean nodded. He gently grasped her elbow, and a weird current shot through his hand and up his arm. His fingertips burned and he met her gaze, wondering if she'd experienced the same kind of unexpected reaction. He looked for a sign, saw nothing and then figured he was imagining things.

"Want to go to the bar?"

She looked dubious and suspicious, and for one nerve-racking moment, he thought she might refuse. But after a second she nodded and walked with him across the foyer. He glanced toward his brothers and saw they were watching him, clearly curious and obviously surprised by his actions. But to their credit, they remained where they were.

"Why are your brothers all lined up and watching you?" she asked, and Sean realized she was the kind of woman who noticed *every* little thing. "Liam looks like he's about to burst a blood vessel."

His plan appeared to be blowing up in his face, but Sean kept walking. "I didn't realize you were on a first-name basis with my brothers."

"I told you I was acquainted with your mother and Kayla, and that I've met Liam several times, since I'm working on an art piece in the foyer of his hotel. And Kieran was on call in the ER when Dad had his stroke."

Of course that made sense. But as Sean mulled over whether he was doing the right thing, involving someone he was inadvertently connected to, a pair of well-dressed cowboys gave her a long and clearly appreciative glance as they passed. Sean couldn't resist glaring back. His ego was healthy enough to cope with a little competition. Not that he was interested in Leah in *that* way. He needed her help for a few minutes, that was all.

It wasn't anything else.

She wasn't his type.

Yeah. Right.

Leah called herself all kinds of foolish as she walked into the restaurant with Sean O'Sullivan. A drink. And a favor. She should have turned on her heel and left the hotel. But her curiosity was piqued. And since she'd already decided that she didn't like him in the least, it wasn't as though she had anything to lose or gain by agreeing to his request.

By the time they reached the bar, he had released her elbow, but her skin still tingled. He didn't blink when she asked for a ridiculously expensive cocktail she knew she'd never drink and ordered a bourbon straight for himself. There were a few people sitting in the bar, but he escorted her toward one of the booths, clearly wanting a little privacy. Once they were seated, she placed her notepad and tape on the table and spoke.

"So, you said you wanted a favor."

He rested his elbows on the table between them. "This *is* the favor."

Leah wasn't convinced. "I thought you were about to ask me to keep the noise down in my studio, or something like that. I've been working on a few new pieces. I know the welding and soldering make a whole lot of noise."

He shrugged lightly. "I haven't noticed the noise."

Leah angled her head and studied him for a moment. He really was remarkably attractive—even with his overlong hair and scruffy half beard. His eyes were a clear, crystalline blue, and he had unfairly long lashes. He wore jeans, a dark shirt and a black leather jacket that fitted his broad shoulders like a glove, and she suspected he had his clothes tailored. There was nothing *off-the-rack* about Sean O'Sullivan.

"So, maybe you'd like to explain this *favor* thing?"

"Not really," he said.

Leah raised one brow. "Being cryptic isn't charming, if that's what you think."

Their drinks arrived, and she stared at the multicolored concoction for a second. Once the waiter disappeared, he responded. "I've never had any complaints before."

Yes, she could believe that!

He was the kind of man her friends would clamor to be with—rich, handsome and sexier than sin. But Leah wasn't about to be bowled over by his good looks or blue eyes. She knew who he was. *What* he was. And since she was so far from being his type, as history had proven, she had no intention of going another round in the humiliation stakes. He wanted something though…and she intended to find out what it was.

"You can save the sexy one-liners," she retorted. "And tell me the truth."

His gaze darkened, and she wondered if he knew the effect that look had on women. On her. The last time they had been this close and in this place, he'd charmed her with a smile and some off-the-cuff comment about her hair, before asking what her friend would like to drink. Yeah, he was all charm, all right. The absurdity of the situation made her chuckle, and she saw his immediate frown.

"Is something funny?"

Leah pushed the ridiculous looking drink aside. "I was just thinking about the last time we were here together."

He jerked back and frowned. "The last time? I don't understand what you—"

"Over there," she said and jerked a thumb vaguely in the direction of the bar. "I was in town visiting my mom and dad over the Christmas break. I'd brought my roommate from college, and we came here for a drink. You were sitting at the bar with some friends and came over to talk to me."

"I did?"

"You did," she said and gave a brittle laugh. "You asked me what kind of drink my friend liked."

He looked…a little embarrassed. "I did?" he said again.

Leah nodded. "Yeah…then you spent the week-end with her in this very hotel."

He shook his head, clearly confused. "I'm sorry, I don't remember who you—"

"That's because you have a reputation for forget-ting women after you get them into bed," she said, cutting him off. "Her name was Carissa, and she was tall and blond with legs up to here," Leah said, holding a hand flat up to her own neck. "You know, your *go-to* type."

He leaned forward on the table, and Leah expe-rienced an odd sensation in her belly. She couldn't help noticing how he stared at her mouth. It was a habit of his. And not one she could honestly say she disliked. There was something about him that was impossible to ignore. Something, she figured, that was responsible for the butterflies in her stomach.

"You think you know my type?"

"Well," she said, and wiggled the fingers on one hand dismissively, "I know it's not someone like me. Which brings me back to my question about this *favor* you said you wanted."

He rested his chin on the back of his hands, calmly ignoring her question. "So, this friend of yours… Ca-rissa…is she still a friend?"

Leah waved a hand vaguely. "She married straight out of college and moved to Texas."

"She came to LA," he said, as a memory clearly kicked in, and then shrugged one broad shoulder. "If I recall correctly, she left after a few days."

Leah's brows rose. "I think she quickly figured you weren't the relationship type. Sorry to say she wasn't pining after you once you returned to Los Angeles. At least, not for very long."

He laughed unexpectedly, and the sound made her insides roll over. *Damn, snap out of it, girl.* She wondered if he had any idea how sexy he was, and then figured he was probably the least self-aware man she'd ever met.

"I'm glad to hear it," he said and grinned. "Pining after anything is such a waste of energy."

"Smooth *and* smug," she said and twirled the umbrella in her unwanted drink. "That's quite a combination."

"Are you always this obnoxious on a date?"

Leah's eyes widened. "Oh…we're on a date now? Five minutes ago you wanted a favor. Now it's a date. Thanks for the heads-up."

She could have sworn she saw color creep up his neck as he sat back in the seat. "Okay…fair enough. I'll explain."

Leah nodded. "I'm listening."

He sighed impatiently. "I was upstairs talking with my brothers, and then they started asking me questions about my decision to return to Cedar River."

"And?"

"And I wanted to get them off my back. When I saw you in the lobby, I thought…" He shrugged again. "I figured they'd get off my case if they believed I was meeting someone for a drink or…whatever."

Whatever? No need to guess what that meant. She remembered how his three siblings were observing them curiously as they had crossed the foyer. "So I'm what…a diversion?"

He actually managed to look a little sheepish. "Well…yeah."

Leah's jaw tightened. "You can't simply tell them to stay the hell out of your business?"

"They're my family. And sometimes family doesn't understand boundaries."

"So you'd rather involve me in this situation than sort it out for yourself?"

He scowled, clearly irritated that she was making a big deal out of it. "It's a drink…not a marriage proposal."

"I'm glad to hear it," she retorted, echoing the words he'd said only moments earlier. "But I'm really not in the mood for either."

She began to slide across the booth seat, but stopped when his hand came across the table and he grasped her wrist. His touch was light and nonthreatening, the look on his face almost pleading— and her skin began to tingle in a way that made her awareness of him skyrocket.

God, I'm stupid.

"Leah, I really—"

The way he said her name made her madder than hell. It didn't matter how many sparks were flying in the moment—he had no right to use her to avoid his family. It was humiliating. And she'd suffered enough humiliation over the past few years.

She shook off his hand and got to her feet. "If you are worried about your family overstepping, don't give them a reason to, O'Sullivan. Don't shack up in that big house by the river with only your misery for company." Leah grabbed her notepad and tape and took a step back, meeting his gaze head-on. "And get a haircut."

Leah ignored the hurt churning in her belly. She took one last look at his startled expression and quickly turned on her heel and fled.

Chapter Three

The one thing Sean missed about California was the weather. Cold had never been his thing. As he trudged up the narrow path from the river, fighting with a few low-hanging branches, he thought about warm summers at the beach. He thought about the friends he'd left, the huge house he'd sold, the career he'd traded for his solitude.

But he had to admit he liked it back here, too, even if the cold weather wasn't to his liking. In the spring it was picture-perfect. From the small jetty by the water's edge, he had a clear view of the river. His brother Liam owned a place half a mile down the river, and along with several other neighboring homes, the entire area was private and peaceful. He simply had to get used to his new life. He had family and several friends from high school in Cedar River, and he had time. Plenty of it. It wasn't as though he had to rush into some new career. He was thirty-two years old and had money in the bank…what was the hurry?

As he left the footpath and found the clearing that led back to the house, he stopped in his tracks, suddenly not feeling the least bit peaceful.

Because two yellow dogs were lying on his porch.

Leah's dogs.

Sean trudged toward the house, mindful that the ground was damp and slippery. He got a couple of yards from the porch, and the lazy hounds lifted their heads and whined in greeting and then promptly went back to sleep.

Sean called the dogs to heel, but it took several minutes to get them down the steps. He didn't bother finding a rope to lead them, since they obediently began following him the moment he began to head through the hedge and toward the Petrovic house. It was early Saturday afternoon, and he knew Ivan was at his usual weekend book club meeting for the first time since his stroke. Which meant Sean had to suck up his reluctance to face Leah again.

Hell. He owed her an apology and he knew it. He'd been out of line at the hotel earlier that week, and her words had given him plenty to think about.

He walked along the path and through the hedge and saw that the shed doors were open and then stopped walking when he reached the doorway. The two dogs remained by his feet, seeming content to stay with him, and he had a vague thought that the hounds had become quite comfortable in his presence.

He stuck his head around the door and spotted Leah immediately. In bright red overalls and a long, knitted coat, her hair falling down her back and large protective glasses shielding her eyes, she looked quite different. Less like the quirky girl next door he was used to...no, she seemed in her element. Powerful.

Sexy.

He dismissed the notion immediately. He didn't like Leah. To imagine her being sexy in any kind of way was just stupid. Still, the idea lingered as he watched her work. She had a small mallet in her hand and was beating a narrow piece of metal into a shallow curve, bending and then flexing the material to create the shape she wanted. He watched for a moment, noticing how intensely she concentrated on her task.

It was intriguing to watch her at work. He'd always admired creativity, it's what had drawn him to the music industry so long ago. As a kid he'd learned to play the piano, as a teenager he gotten his first guitar—even though he preferred being behind the microphone rather than in front of it. He'd been in a band in high school and still enjoyed playing the guitar. Watching Leah work her magic on the metal in her hands had an almost mesmerizing effect on him. He shook the feeling off and pushed some action into his legs. By the time he was a few feet from her, she was aware of his presence and had flipped the glasses onto her head, staring at him.

Long and hard.

Her inspection made him smile and he crossed his arms, leaning carefully against one of the workbenches, waiting for her to speak.

She bit down a little on her bottom lip and tilted her head a fraction, inspecting him without hiding the fact. "Better."

Sean raised his brows. "You think?"

"Well," she said and motioned to his jaw. "Now the world can see all of your pretty face."

He'd gotten a haircut and shaved off the beard two days ago, but her words made him laugh. "You know, that's not exactly the look I was going for."

She shrugged slightly. "I'm sure your ego is healthy enough to take it." She turned away for a moment and ditched the glasses and mallet. When she swiveled back, she was frowning. "So?"

Sean realized he'd missed something she'd said, and a familiar uneasiness at his failing hearing quickly curled up his spine. "What?"

"I said," she replied and walked around the workbench, "what can I do for you?"

Sean straightened up and moved closer. Time to get it over with. "I wanted to…" His words trailed off, and he let out a heavy sigh. "I…"

"Well," she prompted, hands on hips. "What?"

"I'm sorry, okay?" he said quickly. "My behavior the other day was crappy."

"You're right," she said. "It was."

Irritation crept up the back of his neck. Damn, the woman knew how to push his buttons. But she had every reason to be mad at him. Now he knew they'd met before; he racked his memory banks and *did* vaguely recall meeting her all those years ago— when she'd said he'd faked interest in her to get to her friend. There'd been a lot of women in his life over the last decade. Too many to count. He couldn't remember faces, let alone names. And her college roommate with the long legs hadn't stuck with him over the years. Of course, he remembered her now, but on reflection the casualness of their hookup wasn't something he was particularly proud of. But he couldn't change the past.

"I'm not usually such a jerk."

She looked skeptical. "I guess time will tell."

The heat crawling up his neck smacked him squarely in the cheeks, and he cleared his throat. "Well, anyway, I'm sorry. And I brought your dogs back. They seem to like hanging out on my porch."

She smiled, and the action unexpectedly made his insides flip over. Sean couldn't understand his reaction to her. She wasn't his type. Far from it. But she did something to him.

"Life by the river obviously suits them," she said and then whistled for the dogs to come into the barn.

"But if they're getting in the way, I'll keep them inside so they don't bother you."

"They don't bother me," he said quickly, realizing that he'd been very clear to himself that they *were* bothering him, and he didn't understand why she had him so tongue-tied that he couldn't admit to the fact. The dogs rushed into the barn and began curling around his legs. Damned animals wouldn't leave him alone. "I mean, I'd hate them to wander off too far from home."

"I'm sure they won't. But I'll keep a closer eye on them in future." She looked at the dogs, and her lips curved up. "They do seem to like you."

His skin got hotter, even though it was a cold morning. "Yeah. So, I guess I'll see you around."

"Dad said you missed your chess game yesterday?" she queried, hands now on her hips.

Sean shrugged. "I was busy. Anyway, he wins every time."

She grinned. "I can show you how to beat him."

Sean was instantly suspicious. "Why would you do that?"

"Because I take pity on your bad moves."

He laughed, certain there was nothing intentionally flirtatious about her words, but they still had that effect. "I think your dad wins because he cheats."

"Haven't you ever been really good at something?"

Sean rocked back, having the crazy thought that she was suddenly being deliberately inflammatory...

almost provocative. He was being foolish. Imagining things simply because he'd been off the dating grid for a long time now. He wasn't used to having a lack of female company…platonic or otherwise. *Not* that he was renowned for having platonic relationships.

"I'm good at things," he said quietly. "Want me to prove it?"

She rolled her eyes. "You can save the pickup routine for someone else, Sean. We both know I'm not your type. And frankly, you're not mine."

"I'm not?"

She laughed. "Don't look so offended. We all have a type, right?"

Sean nodded. "I suppose."

"Well, you like tall blondes with long legs, correct?"

He wasn't about to tell her that he preferred brunettes. "Sure. And you?"

"Well, history might suggest that I like the charming, shallow type. But now that I've moved back home, I've made a conscious decision to do the opposite of everything I've done in the past. Case in point—find charming, egotistical men attractive."

"So, you had your heart broken?" Sean asked.

"Hearts," she corrected, and held up two fingers. "Two jackasses in my past. What about you?"

Sean figured there was no point in being coy. "No broken heart."

"Oh, I get it…you don't let anyone in," she said bluntly. "Afraid of being hurt?"

He shrugged. "Not at all."

"Cynical, then," she said, regarding him curiously. "Not sure you believe in all that romantic nonsense?"

"So you admit that it's nonsense?"

"Romance?" she queried. "I've haven't had much luck with the concept. Like I said, I have a history of choosing badly, and in my meager experience men use romance to get sex."

"And women use sex to get romance," he added. "Isn't that what they say?"

She shrugged slightly. "Probably. For the moment I'm fine concentrating on my dad and my work."

Sean ignored the twitch in his belly, which he figured had *nothing* to do with the fact he was discussing sex and romance with a woman he barely knew. She'd moved around the workbench and he followed, ensuring that he could hear what she said.

"I like your dad," he said.

Her mouth curled at the edges. "He likes you, too," she replied. "Not sure why though."

Sean chuckled. "There you go, still thinking the worst of me."

"Absolutely."

He ignored her reply, and gestured to the metal she'd been working on earlier. "Tell me about your work."

Her gaze narrowed, but after a moment her shoulders relaxed a little. "It's part of the piece I'm doing for the foyer at your hotel."

"Liam's hotel," he corrected.

"Same name on the stationary," she noted, brows up.

Sean dismissed the twitch between his shoulder blades. "What's your inspiration?"

"This place," she replied and waved a hand. "This town. The people. The history. Before it became a tourist stopover with holiday dude ranches and bus tours, Cedar River was once a thriving mining community. I'd like to reflect that, while respecting the relationship between the original occupants of the area, and the land. The Black Hills are sacred to the Lakota Sioux people and I feel I have a responsibility to make sure that is reflected in what I do." She shrugged lightly. "It's a work in progress, I guess."

He was impressed by her passion and couldn't help thinking how lovely she looked with her hair falling down her back. And her perfume unexpectedly reached him—some kind of spicy, vanilla scent he found pleasant assailed his senses. Perhaps it wasn't even perfume and more likely her shampoo, but he discovered that he liked it and moved a little closer. For the first time, he noticed that her eyes had a darker ring around the iris, highlighting the vivid green color.

"Have I got something on my face?"

Her voice was soft and husky and barely audible, but still he heard it clearly enough to jerk his thoughts back to the moment. "Ah…no. I was just… I was thinking…"

She propped her hands on her hips and laughed softly. "Tell me something, does this sexy staring thing you do generally work for you? It's almost like you watch when someone speaks, rather than listen. It's very…intense."

Sean's spine straightened. She was so close to the truth. Too close. He found some solace in watching people speak, even if he couldn't always hear them. It was unnerving that she'd noticed, and at the same time oddly comforting. He felt ridiculous even thinking it, but still, the idea lingered as he watched her.

"You're still doing it," she remarked, smiling.

Sean's insides jolted. "Sorry."

She nodded. "I was about to head inside and make coffee. Coming?"

It was more of a demand than an invitation, but he nodded and followed her from the shed and toward the house. Sean had been inside Ivan's home many times and traced her steps through the back door, through the mudroom and into the large kitchen. There was a big scrubbed oak table in the room, surrounded by matching chairs and an old-fashioned dresser with its mix of china and glassware and collection of old jugs.

"Sean?"

Her voice, louder than usual, got his thoughts back on track. "What?"

She came around the counter and placed the mugs on the table. "I asked if you want cream and sugar?"

"Neither," he replied and sat down.

She pulled out a chair and dropped into it. "Can I ask you something else?"

it hasn't anything to do with me. I just told him to get a haircut."

Gwen smiled. "I love all my kids equally. But Sean is my youngest and my—"

"Favorite?" Leah suggested and smiled.

The older woman shrugged. "The last one is always the hardest to let go. And he was so determined to make his own way in the world when he was eighteen… I guess I feel as though I've missed so much of his life because he's lived so far away. And now that he's back, I just want keep him close."

"Well, he bought a house, so it appears that he's here to stay."

He bought my house.

She ignored the twitch racing over her skin when she thought about him being in the big home by the river. Leah knew her feelings were irrational—he couldn't have known she wanted to buy the place. But her resentment lingered.

"You're probably right," Gwen said and moved around the counter. "I worry too much. Perhaps because Liam and Kieran have gotten married I feel as though he's spending too much time alone. Or maybe I'm just intrigued by the idea of more grandchildren someday," she added and smiled.

Leah couldn't miss the innuendo. "Don't read anything into it. He brought my dogs home after they were caught lounging on his porch," she said and began pulling food out of the refrigerator. "To be honest, I reckon your son thinks I'm

A cautionary wall rose up immediately. "Sure."

She placed her elbows on the table. "Why did you really leave California?"

"I wanted to come home to spend more time with my family." They were the same words he'd voiced many times since he'd returned to Cedar River. "Like I said."

"You don't strike me as the family man kind of guy," she said flatly. "From reputation alone you clearly have had a successful life in the *fast lane,* and Cedar River is a world away from that. Why the sudden change?"

Sean was about to begin his usual spiel about taking a break and reshifting his focus when he saw her attention suddenly diverted from him and toward the back door. Moments later Ivan Petrovic came through the mudroom and into the kitchen. Two seconds later he realized that Ivan wasn't alone. A woman was behind him, her tall stature and silvery hair instantly recognizable.

Mom.

Since she'd first met Gwen O'Sullivan, Leah had been drawn to the other woman. She was tall and strikingly elegant, a kind, warm person who possessed a compassionate, caring nature and was well regarded within the community. She'd handled herself throughout the very public separation and divorce from her husband of thirty-five years with reserve and self-respect. Leah knew her ex-husband

had since married the woman with whom he'd se-
cretly had a child thirty-two years earlier. It was a
complicated situation, but Gwen appeared to be cop-
ing with everything as well as could be expected—at
least that's what Leah's father had told her. And as
she watched her dad and Gwen walk into the kitchen,
Leah suspected there was definitely more to their
budding friendship than her dad was letting on.

She glanced at Sean and saw the surprise and
then suspicion in his expression. Damn, he was as
handsome as the devil. Clean-shaven and sport-
ing a short hairstyle, in jeans and a black shirt that
stretched across his broad shoulders, and a leather
aviator jacket, he looked like he'd stepped out of a
sexy cologne ad. And suddenly, an old and deliberately forgotten longing rumbled throughout her
blood. She pushed it back, unwilling to go there because it was stupid and futile, and she wasn't the
kind of woman to waste time when it came to men.
At least not anymore.

"Hi, Dad. Hello, Mrs. O'Sullivan," she said and
pushed back the chair as she got to her feet.

The older woman smiled. "Oh, call me Gwen,"
she insisted and then glanced toward her son, smiling broadly. "Hello, darling."

His mouth twitched at the sweet endearment, and
Leah had to fight the laughter bubbling in her throat,
waiting for him to speak. "Hi, Mom."

"It's good to see you."

It was a pointed remark, and everyone in the room
knew it.

Sean shrugged. "You, too."

"I wasn't expecting to see you here."

His jaw tensed. "Likewise."

"You got a haircut," Gwen said and moved around
the table. "Good."

Leah looked at her dad, saw that he was smiling and he winked at her. And then she laughed.
great guffaw that had both the O'Sullivans star-
at her. Gwen chuckled. Her dad grinned. And S
scowled, clearly unhappy that his mother app
to be keeping company with Leah's father.

"I was about to make lunch," Leah said and
back behind the counter. "Would you like to

She saw that Sean was about to get t
and refuse the invitation, until Gwen pla
tle hand on his shoulder, pressing him b
seat. "We'd like that very much, than
why don't you keep Ivan company in th
for a while and I'll help Leah."

He did a little grumbling as he
and by then her father was halfway
Gwen shooed Sean the rest of the w
were finally alone, the older won

"Thank you."

Leah shook her head. "For

"For getting him out of tha
circulation."

Her mouth twisted. "If he

Gwen laughed. "At least you've got him thinking."

Leah's cheeks scorched. "Ah...yes...well... I should probably get this lunch organized."

"Sure, what can I do to help?"

They spent the following minutes making a pile of sandwiches and a fresh pot of coffee, setting the table and pulling out her father's favorite plates. Leah watched as Gwen moved around the room and realized it wasn't the first time the older woman had been in her dad's kitchen.

"So," she said as casually as she could manage. "You and my dad, huh?"

Gwen looked up from her task. "We're friends."

Leah wasn't convinced that it was strictly friendship. "That's good. He needs a friend."

The other woman met her gaze levelly. "We all do. Even Sean, despite how much he thinks he doesn't need anyone. I don't think he's quite forgiven his father for everything that happened."

"You mean Jonah?" Leah asked quietly.

Gwen shrugged a little. "Jonah gets the brunt of Sean's blame because he's the product of my ex-husband's infidelity. And they were born just three months apart. But it's not Jonah's fault. It's not anyone's fault. It just...*is*."

Leah admired the other woman's innate strength, but she also understood Sean's lingering resentment. "I guess no one likes to see their parents split up."

"You're right. But J.D. has moved on with his life..."

"And so have you?" Leah suggested and smiled. "Which is great. My dad is a wonderful man."

"Who's very set in his ways," Gwen offered wryly. "And we really are just friends. I'm not sure either of us is inclined to think of one another as anything more. But friendships are important for us all. In a way I suppose you're also starting your life over again." She nodded. "Making new friends...opening yourself up to possibilities."

Leah wondered what kind of possibilities the other woman meant, and when she saw that Gwen was smiling, knew immediately. "You're way off the mark."

She shrugged. "Perhaps it's just wishful thinking. I'd like to see my son happy and settled, with someone who genuinely cares for him."

Leah almost laughed out loud. "Well, if I see any tall, leggy blondes in town, I'll send them his way."

"Window dressing," Gwen said and waved a hand. "What he needs is someone grounded and honest who doesn't tell him how wonderful he is every second of the day or night. So, if you know anyone like that, introduce her, will you?"

As far as Leah was concerned, she was as far away from being Sean O'Sullivan's type as anyone could be—and she was okay with that. But having his mother's obvious approval, particularly when she was barely acquainted with the man, was too ridiculous for words. And Leah had too much else going on in her life to waste time on a guy who wasn't her type. Including get involved with anyone—and certainly not with her neighbor.

"Okay," she said agreeably and ignored the way her heart pounded in her chest. "I'll try to remember."

Gwen laughed softly. "You're a nice girl, Leah. And I don't mean to be pushy or meddlesome."

"Sure you do."

The older woman laughed again. "Of course, you're right. It's a mother's natural instinct to see her chicks happy. And I want to see Sean as happy as his brothers are. He needs a family of his own."

Leah's body tingled in spectacular fashion.

Idiot.

"I'm sure he'll manage that for himself when he's ready."

Gwen's mouth curled into a smile. "I'm not so sure. I think I might need to make him see sense. But, since I also think I've embarrassed you enough for one afternoon, I promise not to mention it again. Anyway, I did want to talk to you about the gallery— perhaps an exhibition is exactly what you need right now."

A familiar uneasiness settled in her veins. Leah knew she needed to get past her fear of rejection when it came to her work. It had become an albatross around her neck since she'd created her first piece. One disastrous gallery showing, two failed relationships and sporadic financial success meant her muse and confidence had taken a battering over the years. She hoped that being in Cedar River would help overcome her anxiety, but she certainly wasn't going to push her boundaries too much, too soon.

"Maybe," she replied. "I'll let you know."

"How are the preparations coming for your brother's wedding?"

"Good," she replied and smiled. "It's going to be at the Triple C. I'm a bridesmaid."

"I'm sure it will be a lovely occasion. Weddings really are a wonderful way of bringing families together."

Leah sighed. She was so happy for her brother. And a little melancholy for herself. One day she hoped to find that same happiness. Someone to love. Someone who loved her in return. It didn't seem like a huge ask…and yet in the past, love had left her broken and betrayed.

Ten minutes later both men were back in the kitchen, and they were all sitting around the table, eating and talking. At least her father and Gwen were talking. Leah half listened to their conversation. The remainder of her attention was focused on Sean and the way he silently ate and seemed to regard them all with a kind of wariness. Leah was usually adept at reading people's moods. But Sean was hard to read. In fact, he was as closed up as a clam.

"Jeez, Sean," she said when there was a break in the conversation, smiling a little as she met his gaze. "A person can't get a word in edgewise with you chattering on all the time."

Gwen and her father laughed, and Leah sipped her coffee.

"Maybe I'm not as fascinated by the sound of my own voice as you are," he said, brows up slightly, his attention shifting to the empty plate in front of him.

Leah got to her feet, her cheeks burning, figuring that if she was going to dish it out she needed to learn to take it also. But still, he made her mad with his quiet disapproval and indifference. She made noises about cleaning up, and Gwen volunteered Sean to help before taking Ivan and their coffee into the living room.

Once they were alone, Leah spoke. "You don't have to help."

He was looking at her. "Apparently I do," he said, then stood, collecting the plates. He came around the counter, placed the dishes in the sink and turned toward Leah. "Ah… I'm sorry about what I said before."

"You are?"

He sighed. "I think I'm a little out of practice being around people."

Leah looked at him. "Well, if it's any consolation, I have been known to be a little too direct at times."

He met her gaze. "Nothing wrong with that. Beats being a moody recluse."

"Is that what you've become?" she asked bluntly.

His mouth flattened and then he grinned a fraction. "According to my brothers."

Leah smiled. "Well, family can be unintentionally critical."

"I guess. Is yours?"

She nodded and half shrugged. "Sometimes they like to tell me how to live my life."

"And here I was thinking you danced to the beat of your own drum."

She smiled again. "I do...mostly. But there are times Dad and my brother like to offer advice about things I should do."

"Such as?"

Conscious that she had him talking—no mean feat according to his mother—Leah told him the truth. "About my career. I get stage fright, you know, about the idea of showing my work."

His expression narrowed. "Yet you're doing a piece for the hotel foyer? Which loads of people will see?"

"Yes," she replied. "But that's not the same as having a showing at a gallery and asking people to turn up and like what they see and potentially buy something."

"But then the world misses out on seeing something beautiful, don't they?" he queried, and grabbed a tea towel. "Self-doubt happens to a lot of creative people. I've seen quite a few well-known stars take a ride on the self-doubt train. The hard part is pushing past it, in believing in your talent and taking a breath and saying, 'I got this.' It takes practice, that's all."

Leah stood motionless, watching him, realizing that he understood exactly what she was feeling, because he had spent over a decade in an industry rife with both ego and hesitation and had clearly encountered both those things. "Thank you."

He waved a dismissive hand. "So, what's the story with your dad and my mom?"

"Story?" she echoed, and opened the dishwasher. "Apparently they're friends."

He didn't look convinced. "Friends? That's it?"

She heard his disapproval, figured it had everything to do with her father, and her protective instincts instantly kicked in. "You know, they're adults. They can do what they like. I wouldn't get your undies in a knot over it, if I were you," she said baldly, and grinned. "You've got bigger problems to worry about."

He stilled. "I do?"

"Yeah," she retorted, hands on hips. "You do."

He was so close she could feel the heat emanating from him. "What problems?"

"Your mom thinks you need a wife."

He rocked back on his heels. "A what?"

"A wife," she repeated, fascinated as a ruddy color crawled up his neck.

He was now scowling so hard she thought his face

might crack. "And does she have anyone in particular in mind?"

She nodded. "Yes."

He looked incredulous. "Who?"

Leah smiled, feeling ridiculously triumphant, and then strangely uncomfortable, because he looked so out of sorts. "Me."

Chapter Four

Sean had no intention of being set up by his mother. And certainly not with Leah. Anyone could see she wasn't his type. Except…she was surprisingly easy to talk to, and he was discovering he liked talking to her. Hanging out with his brothers had become a chore, since all they wanted to do was tell him how to live his life. But Leah was refreshingly candid and funny and had a way of making him forget his troubles.

"I'm sorry she's doing that," he said and grabbed a dish, thinking how he'd never been one for domestic chores, but didn't mind washing up with Leah. "My mom thinks all her kids need to settle down."

"Well, since Liam, Kieran and Jonah all got married in the last few years, you probably can't blame her for wanting that for you, too."

"Maybe," he said. "Although I'm not sure I'm wired that way."

"What way?" she asked. "For marriage?"

"Some people aren't the marrying kind."

"I suppose. Were you one of those kids who didn't like sharing his toys in the sandbox?"

Sean listened to her poking fun, and strangely, didn't mind. He figured he owed her the odd poke, considering some of the things he'd said to her since they'd met. "I know how to share. But marriage and kids are… I don't know…about a big a commitment as a person can get. And frankly, I've seen too many lousy marriages to believe in fairy tales."

"Your parents?" she asked bluntly.

He half shrugged. "Yeah. And LA doesn't exactly have the reputation for creating actual happily-ever-afters. Only make-believe."

She nodded. "I suppose. But your brothers all have happy relationships now, right?"

"Yeah, sure."

"And *my* folks were very happy."

He regarded her soberly for a moment. "Your mom's death must have been a terrible shock for your family."

"It was," she replied and nodded. "And poor David lost his wife, Jayne, in the same accident. She was the pilot. It was aircraft mechanical failure," she added with a sigh. "A freak accident no one could have predicted."

"Your brother has met someone else now, hasn't he?"

"Yes, Annie," she explained. "She was the nanny for his kids, and after a few years they fell in love. Scarlett and Jasper adore her, and I've never seen my brother so happy. Actually, their wedding is next week."

"So, you're saying that marriage is a good idea?"

She smiled. "For some. Not that I have any experience with it. Maybe I'm like you and not the marrying kind."

Sean rested his hip against the counter. They were close enough that he could hear her quite clearly. "Oh, I'm sure some local cowboy will snatch you up."

Leah's brow rose quizzically. "Do I look like the cowboy type?"

Sean grinned. "Maybe. Don't all girls like a cowboy?"

"My last *failed* relationship," she said, and put the word in air quotes, "was with a slick city boy who wore a fake Armani watch and lied his ass off the whole time we were together. Oh, did I mention that he stole most of my money, too," she added, and smiled, but Sean didn't see any laughter behind her eyes—only pain and betrayal.

"So he was a worthless jerk?"

She nodded. "By the time the police caught up

with him, he'd lost the money at a casino. I should have seen through him, I suppose. He was way too good-looking to be interested in me."

"What?" Sean looked shocked. "Why would you say such a thing?"

She shrugged. "Beautiful people usually like other beautiful people."

Sean grinned. "I'm not sure that's true."

"Oh, it's true all right," she said, looking directly at him. "Xavier told me as much before he took off with my savings. I'd wager that your last girlfriend was either an actress or a model."

"As a matter of fact, she was a landscape architect," he replied, remembering Cindy fondly. True, she had done some modeling, but when Sean met her she was working in her own business designing gardens for some of Bel Air's rich and famous. Unfortunately, their relationship had waned after a few months. The usual scenario, since commitment wasn't exactly his forte.

"Really?" Leah said, her expression exaggerated. "I'm impressed."

"Maybe I'm not the shallow, predictable jerk you pegged me for."

"Maybe. What she tall, blond and pretty?"

"Yes."

Leah made a face. "With legs up to here?" she asked, and held a palm flat to her shoulders. "And endowed with great…ah…assets?"

Sean grinned and nodded. "Okay. Maybe I *am* a shallow jerk after all."

"Don't feel bad," she said and tossed the dishcloth onto the draining board. "I'm sure you're in good company with nearly every other man on the planet."

"Ouch," he said and winced. "The slick city boy certainly did a number on you."

She nodded. "He certainly did. There are only two men I trust...my father and my brother. What about you?" she asked and regarded him levelly. "Who has your back? Your brothers?"

Sean thought about her question for a moment and then shrugged. "I guess. Except when they're telling me how to live my life. Which they seem to be doing a lot lately."

"Gotta love family, right? What about your friends from LA...don't you miss them?"

"Some," he admitted. "But the truth is, it was easier to leave it all behind than I'd have thought. Maybe the people I thought were friends were more like acquaintances." He shrugged. "Or maybe I'm just an unfriendly ass who's become way too used to being alone since coming home."

"You're not alone now though," she reminded him and smiled. "And you know, when you try, you're actually okay to be around. Even likable."

Sean grinned. "Does this mean we're becoming friends?"

"Why not? Most of us could use one or two more."

Sean met her gaze. A female friend—and not

someone he was thinking about getting into bed. He liked the idea. And not that he *wasn't* thinking about Leah that way. The truth was, he did find her attractive and easy to be around. She had a warmth about her that drew him in. Sure, they argued and disagreed, but underneath their mutual antagonism, something else stirred between them. Attraction maybe? Awareness? Lust?

Where did that come from?

"I have to get going," he said and straightened. "Thanks for lunch. I'll see my mom on the way out."

Sean quickly left the kitchen, heading for the living room. He saw his mother and Ivan sitting together on the couch—she was laughing at something Ivan said. Annoyance seeped through his blood as he watched them for moment, thinking about his family, about his brothers and how they'd both settled into marriage and family life. And he thought about his father and how J.D. was happier than he'd ever seen him now that he was married to Kathleen. And he thought about Jonah, too. And about how much resentment he felt for his half brother—a resentment he knew was irrational and still couldn't ignore. It was as though his whole family had moved on. And now even his mother was finding a new life for herself. He turned from the scene and headed out the door toward the path through the hedge.

Somehow, Sean had thought that coming home to Cedar River would have felt more familiar…but nothing was as he had imagined. So, he remained apart from them, keeping a safe distance, convinced he didn't fit in with their lives and there was no place for him within the frame of his family. Perhaps he'd simply stayed away too long. Or hadn't visited enough.

Back at his house, Sean figured spending the rest of the afternoon alone was a good idea. He grabbed a novel he had intended reading months ago and tried to relax in front of the fire for a while, but by four o'clock he was wandering around the big house, going from room to room. Maybe he needed to renovate the place. It would give him something to do. Although he would have to hire contractors to do anything significant, since he hadn't picked up a paintbrush or a power tool in the last decade.

He received a text from his old school friend, Will Serrato, and when Will invited him to meet up at Rusty's for a drink and a possible game of pool, Sean decided to take him up on it—he had to admit the solitude was getting to him.

He spent the remainder of the afternoon tackling a few of the boxes that were still packed up in one of the spare bedrooms. Junk now, he supposed, looking at the box of awards and accolades he'd gathered over the years. He didn't plan to keep them on display. Being reminded of the career he'd left behind wasn't in his plans. He muttered a curse and taped the box back up, shoving it in the closet.

At seven o'clock, he showered and dressed and grabbed his car keys. He'd kept the fire-engine red

Ferrari when he came home, knowing the thing stood out like a beacon in Cedar River. In LA, it had been nothing out of the ordinary. He should keep it garaged, he supposed, and buy a Jeep or a Ranger like his brothers owned. Certainly the all-wheel drive would be more practical for the local roads. But for the moment, the car was his only set of wheels, so he didn't have a choice. Besides, he enjoyed driving it. Too bad if people thought he was a pretentious ass. People could think what they liked.

He arrived at Rusty's just before eight o'clock. The tavern had been around for decades and now catered to a younger crowd, unlike the Loose Moose, which was family friendly, or the hotel, which he wanted to avoid. He spotted Will sitting at one of the booths. They'd been good friends in high school and had kept in contact over the years. He'd been best man at Will's wedding, and had recommended a lawyer when he'd gotten divorced a few years later.

"Good to see you," Will said and shook his hand. "How's retirement?"

Sean shrugged, realizing the loud music was reverberating in his eardrums, and that hearing Will above the noise was going to be difficult. Maybe meeting at the bar wasn't such a great idea after all. "Boring as hell. How's life on the ranch?"

Will had been foreman at the big Pritchard cattle ranch for years. "Wonderful," he said and made a scoffing sound. "Living the dream."

"Is old man Pritchard still a miserable SOB?"

"Yep," Will replied. "I really need to buy my own place. You know, and get a life," he added, grinning.

He missed something his friend said amid the noise of the crowd and figured the best thing to do was pretend he'd heard. "You still want to raise goats?"

Will made a face, speaking loudly above the music. "You know very well it's alpacas."

"Same thing," Sean replied and laughed. "Just bigger."

"What about you?" his friend queried. "I figured you'd be stir-crazy for the city by now."

"And leave all this?"

Will grinned. "Ah… I saw J.D. the other day. He said he hasn't talked to you much lately."

Sean looked at his friend, struggling to hear as much as he could. "You know how I feel about the situation."

Will nodded. "About your dad? Sure I do. But since losing my mom a couple of years ago, I've realized that time with the people we care about can be short."

Sean knew his friend was right. And he wasn't deliberately ignoring J.D.—he just didn't want to rehash any old resentment. The truth was, he was still mad at his father for lying to them all and then hooking up with Kathleen so soon after separating from his mom.

He looked around, and unexpectedly spotted Leah sitting at the bar with two other women. "Crap."

"What?"

"My neighbor," he explained and sighed.

Will glanced toward the bar. "Which one?"

"In the middle."

His friend grinned. "She's cute. Want me to invite her over?"

"No."

Will was on his feet in a second. "Be back soon."

Sean grimaced and watched as his friend wove through the tables and headed straight for the bar. Sean looked directly ahead, fiddling with the salt shaker, convinced he should bail and leave Will to the trio, since he wasn't in the mood for any kind of socializing. Not so long ago he'd been very much at ease in all social situations. But the more reclusive he became, the more discomfort he experienced when he stepped out of his isolation. He could feel the music beating through his chest, and it filled him with both regret and nostalgia. In that moment he missed his old life more than he had for months. He was about to stand when he felt a soft hand on his arm. He turned his head and saw Leah standing beside the booth. She wore a short, long-sleeved multicolored dress that was cinched at the waist, a long sleeveless suede vest and a pair of high boots. Her amazing hair hung loose over her shoulders, and she had a small tray in her other hand, holding two beers. And damn, she looked hot. So hot that he had to remind himself that he wasn't attracted to her.

"Hi," she said.

"Hello," Sean replied, looking at where her hand lay. She flushed a little and removed it immediately.

"Your friend said you wanted to speak to me," she said and slipped into the seat, pushing a beer toward him. "Cheers."

"Actually," he said, staring at her, "I specifically said I didn't want to see you. But Will likes to cause trouble."

"You can be such a grouch, Sean," she said and grinned. "So, what brings you to Rusty's tonight? The music? The food? The girls?"

He lifted the glass in front of him. "The beer."

She smiled and gestured to the bar, and to where Will was now seated between the two other women. "Looks like your friend has deserted you."

"Just as well I have you to keep me company then."

She laughed, and suddenly it was the only sound he heard above the music and clinking glasses. "I thought you told your friend you didn't want to see me?"

"I did," he replied. "But we both know that's not true. Besides, as you pointed out the other day, if we hang out together as friends it will stop my mom from matchmaking."

"Or make things worse?"

He shrugged. "It's a risk, but I'll take it."

She laughed again. "Well, since I'm not your type, and I've categorically sworn off sex-on-legs guys, I'd say it's a low-end risk."

Sean chuckled. "That's an insult, right?"

"Not exactly. I mean, I'd have to be a rock not to notice how attractive you are. Which I'm not. But I'd be happy to be your friend."

Sean wasn't sure what to feel or think. Being around Leah felt good. "Okay. Friends sounds like a great idea. So, in this new capacity of yours, can you recommend a good contractor?"

She frowned. "What?"

"I want to paint some of the rooms in the house."

"How many rooms?" she asked, her expression softening.

"A couple."

Her steep brows arched higher. "And you want to *hire* a contractor? What, no time to do it yourself?" she asked with bald sarcasm.

Sean shifted in his seat. "I'm not exactly a manual labor kind of guy."

She guffawed. "Now you just sound like a typical O'Sullivan man. An entitled snob," she said bluntly. "I'll tell you what—we'll go to the hardware store together and buy the paint, and *I'll* help you. It'll save you a wad of cash and help remove that thick top layer of city boy you have going on."

Sean laughed. "I can spare the cash…but since you're convinced that I'm useless, I accept your offer."

"Good. How about tomorrow? I made plans for the morning, but I can change them."

"Hot date?"

She laughed. "Horseback riding with my cousin Ellie," she replied, and hooked a thumb in the direction of her friends siting at the bar with Will. "I'll pick you up tomorrow at eight o'clock."

"Don't change your plans. I'll pick *you* up," he corrected. "At twelve o'clock."

She laughed and the image made him smile. There was something refreshingly authentic about Leah. Something that made him want to spend more time with her.

"Not a morning person, are you?"

He leaned forward, struggling to hear her over the music. "Not really. But the real reason is that I promised Kieran I'd drop by his place around ten to help him set up a new surround sound system for the kids."

She nodded. "He's really stepped up to be a good stepdad to his wife's nephews, hasn't he?"

"Yeah," Sean replied. "Kieran's a good man. Why don't you come with me?" he asked, surprising himself.

"Okay," she said agreeably, surprising him further. "Can you pick me up at the Triple C ranch at nine thirty?"

"The Culhane place?"

She nodded. "I am half Culhane, remember," she reminded him. "Is that a problem?"

"Not at all," he said.

"I should get back to my friends," she said and sighed. "And send *your* friend on his way, since both

Ellie and Winona are partial to cowboys and this is meant to be a girls' night out."

"And yet here you are, talking to me."

"Well, I can't help that you're irresistible, can I?" she replied and got to her feet, grabbing the beer before she sauntered back to the bar.

Will returned to the booth seat a minute later. "Whose number did you get—the brunette's or the redhead's?" Sean asked.

"Neither," his friend replied. "I was giving you some time to get your ducks in a row."

"My what?"

"Ducks," Will replied. "Or duck, in the singular. The cute little duck with nice legs and colorful bangs. You didn't mention she was David McCall's little sister. And Mitch Culhane's cousin."

"You didn't ask," Sean said and shrugged. "You know McCall, don't you?"

Will nodded. "Yeah. He's Pritchard's accountant. And Culhane is one of the local brand inspectors, so he comes out to the ranch every now and then. She's not your usual type."

"She not my type at all," he said and sipped his beer, leaning forward again so he could hear his friend speak above the noise around them. "That's why we're just friends."

"Yeah," Will said and laughed. "That's why you haven't stopped staring at her since we arrived."

Sean didn't deny it. But he wasn't about to start thinking about Leah or anyone else in that way. Because if he started something, chances are she would want to know everything about him. And he wasn't in the market to come clean and reveal his innermost hopes and dreams—*or condition*—to anyone. Friends was okay. Friends was enough. Friends was all he had the energy for.

Anything else was off the table.

"So…you're actually going out with Sean O'Sullivan?"

Leah pressed her heels gently against the girth and urged Chico forward. The big overo gelding obliged instantly, and they jogged to catch up with her cousin, Ellie Culhane, who was riding her horse Valiant. She didn't really want to have another discussion about her plans to spend the afternoon with Sean, or why she'd agreed to the idea in the first place. The truth was, she liked him. And once she pushed past his prickles, he was funny and quite charming. "I'm helping him paint his house."

"Why?" Ellie asked and scowled.

Leah shrugged. "Just being neighborly."

"But he's an O'Sullivan," Ellie reminded her. "And Culhanes and O'Sullivans generally don't mix well."

"Since I'm also half Petrovic, I don't think that rule applies. And besides, I'm sure all that old schoolyard tension is forgotten. Sean's brother Kieran looked after my dad when he had his stroke, and if

I remember right, he was the doctor on duty when Mitch had that bad accident last year."

"Well, yeah," Ellie admitted. "Kieran's a good doctor."

"And besides, it's not a date," she added. "We're neighbors now and have sort of become friends." She checked her watch. "Speaking of which, I need to get back."

Leah urged Chico into a lope, and they quickly made their way back to the ranch. When they rode through the gate behind the stables, she spotted a bright red sports car parked in the driveway.

"Nice rig," Ellie said, and laughed as they rode to the hitching rail beside the stables.

A group of chickens scattered as they approached and Leah quickly dismounted, passing Chico's reins to a young ranch hand who appeared at her side. "Thanks," she said and smiled. "He'll need a brush down."

The young man nodded. "Sure thing," he said politely.

Leah waited for Ellie, and they headed for the main house. The Triple C was one of the largest spreads in the area, aside from the O'Sullivan place on the other side of town, and Leah had spent much of her childhood on the ranch. Mitch Culhane bred and raised some of the finest horses in the state, as well as beef cattle. By comparison, her brother's ranch was more of a hobby farm. She spotted her cousin Mitch sitting on the wide porch, and Sean was perched on the balustrade across from him.

"Good morning," she said as she took the steps. Sean was on his feet in a second and greeted her at the top step. "You're early."

"A little." He smiled and Leah's belly flip-flopped. She really had to get a grip. "If you're ready to go, I'll just quickly clean up and grab my bag."

"No hurry," he said agreeably and grinned. "We've got plenty of time."

Leah walked inside and made her way into the downstairs bathroom. She washed up, changed into a new shirt, released her hair from its ponytail and headed back outside. Mitch's wife, Tess, was on the porch, holding their son Charlie, and Ellie was now standing on the top step, clearly laughing at something Sean had said. Stupidly, a little green-eyed monster rose up and tightened her chest, and Leah plastered on her best smile.

"Oh, God, I'm sorry," Ellie said and laughed again. "I said, I bet it's quick, not I bet it's *big*."

"What's going on?" Leah asked cheerfully.

"Nothing," Sean said and unexpectedly moved closer to her. He was smiling, but she sensed a sudden undercurrent of tension to his mood. "Just a flattering misunderstanding."

"About his car," Mitch said and chuckled. Then he reached out to shake Sean's hand. "See you again." He glanced in Leah's direction. "No doubt."

Color smacked her face, and she quickly hugged

Tess and kissed Charlie's head. "Thanks for the loan of Chico."

"The offer's still there to take him to David's," Mitch said and hugged her.

"I can't afford to buy him," she said and sighed. Then she spoke again when her cousin opened his mouth to speak. "And I wouldn't think of accepting him as a gift."

Chico was an extremely valuable horse, and although Mitch had offered the animal to her on several occasions, Leah had no intention of accepting charity—not even from her family.

"Stubborn," Ellie said and grinned, one brow arched.

"Realistic," Leah corrected. "One day maybe." She looked at Sean. "I'm ready."

He nodded. "Sure," he replied, and said goodbye to her family before they headed directly for his car. When the vehicle came into view, Leah raised her brows. "Really…a red Ferrari?"

He shrugged, not looking the least bit embarrassed. "It didn't stick out so much in LA."

Leah laughed. "You know, Sean, your thick skin and monumental ego are oddly likable."

He grinned as he opened the passenger door and gestured for her to get in. "Watch your head," he said, and she ignored the odd sensation whirling around in her belly at the warmth of his voice. She really did need to stop having such out of control reactions to him. They were friends. Nothing more.

The seat, she discovered, was surprisingly comfortable, and there was more legroom that she'd expected.

"Um, where exactly are we going to store the paint and brushes?" she asked as she pushed her tote to her feet.

He didn't respond, and quickly closed the door and moved around to the driver's side. "Seat belt," he instructed.

"You didn't answer my question."

He frowned. "What question?"

"The paint and brushes—where are we going to put them?"

He shrugged and looked away for a moment. "I figured I could get the stuff delivered. If not, I'll drop by the hotel and borrow my brother's Silverado."

"We could have saved you the trouble and gone in my truck."

"You mean that old green jalopy that blows smoke up and down the driveway?"

"I'll have you know I've owned that old jalopy for ten years."

"Then I think it's time for an upgrade," he remarked and started the engine.

The rumble made Leah smile. "I'm not exactly in the market to buy a new car."

"Or a horse," he added and looked her way as he drove away from the house.

"Chico is worth a lot of money," she explained.

"Way more than I could ever pay for him, and I won't take charity from my family."

"Pride?"

"Absolutely," she replied, not hearing any censure in his tone. Somehow, she suspected he understood her motives. She knew he'd taken off for California when he was young to make his own way in the world. He was a man who didn't want to rely on others. Self-sufficient and independent. Much like herself. Perhaps that's why they were beginning to get along—because they understood one another. "Thank you for not calling me a stubborn fool."

"It's not my place to make judgments," he remarked quietly and turned the vehicle onto the road. "Although your extended family seems to care about you a great deal."

"They do," she agreed and sighed. "I think they feel sorry for me."

"Why would you think that?"

"Because I'm the free spirit in the family," she said and laughed. "You know, the one who'll always live from week to week and waste time chasing her dreams."

"Creative people change the world," he said quietly. "Imagine a world without Elvis, or Da Vinci, or Jane Austen. They were all dream-chasers at one point or another."

Leah's throat tightened. "I'm terrified of failing."

"Why?" he asked.

Leah let out a long breath. "I had a manager a few

years back. He was an art dealer and also my boy-friend. He arranged an art showing at a gallery and no one turned up. It was humiliating. Soul destroying. It was like all my dreams, all my work, meant nothing." She sighed heavily. "I guess I'm a coward because I haven't had the courage to try again."

"Understandable," he said. "It takes guts to get back up and go another round. In the music industry I've witnessed a lot of talented people give up, and some not-so-talented people make it big. Persistence is half the battle won. And it sounds like your manager was your biggest problem back then."

She nodded and winced. "We were dating…it made things difficult. And then I found out he was married, and it all turned to into one great disaster after that."

"Well, think of the *right now* as a clean slate. Every now and then we all need one of those."

"Even you?"

He glanced sideways. "Even me."

"Is that why you left LA?"

He loosely shrugged one shoulder. "I had my reasons."

"You know," she said and relaxed in the seat, "friends share things—like I just did when I told you about my ex. And since we've established that we're friends now, I think it's time you came clean."

"No."

"So, you're a hypocrite *and* a crappy friend."

He looked straight ahead, his hands tight on the

steering wheel, a tiny pulse throbbing in his cheek. Leah felt tension rising between them in the small confines of the vehicle and was about to suggest he take her back when he spoke again.

"I don't mean to be."

Leah's insides lurched. There was something achingly vulnerable about the way he said the words and she quickly backpedaled. "Sorry…sometimes I speak before I think. I don't think you're a hypocrite. Or a bad friend. I think you're…"

"What?" he asked as her words trailed off.

"Misunderstood," she replied. "And like me, you don't trust easily."

"I should, I suppose," he said and glanced at her. "Considering the easy ride I had growing up. You know, the rich man's son, who never had to work hard for anything. That's what everyone used to say about me, isn't it?"

"But you did," she reminded him, leaning closer. "You left this town behind and made a very successful life in a new city. You should be really proud of that. I know your mom is."

"She's biased." But he smiled a little.

"Maybe," Leah replied. "She loves you. But she's worried about you, too."

"I know."

"So, maybe you should tell her what's bothering you. Something is. We can all see it."

He didn't say anything for a moment, simply kept driving. She expected him to deny it, to say it was nothing, that she and everyone else were thinking things that were way off base. But finally, after a strained silence, he said, "I can't."

"Why not, Sean?" she asked gently.

"Because they'll... I don't know, smother me and I just... I don't want that."

The pain and frustration in his voice was palpable. Leah sucked in a breath, imagining the worst, that he was sick...or dying. She touched his arm. "Sean, what is it?"

He looked straight ahead, the pulse in his cheek throbbing. "Sometimes... I can't hear you."

She shook her head. "I don't understand."

"Leah," he said and glanced at her. "I'm going deaf."

Chapter Five

Sean had no idea why he told Leah the one thing he didn't want anyone knowing. Maybe because deep down, he actually wanted to tell someone. *Anyone*. And she was the person closest at hand. Or maybe it was because he suspected he wouldn't get sympathy and platitudes and pity from her. Just more questions—which she began firing at him.

"What are you saying?" she asked. "You have a hearing problem?"

"Yes," he replied flatly. "Now can we drop it?"

"Not a chance," she said and stared at him. "Tell me what that means."

Sean sighed heavily and after a few moments pulled the car off the road and onto a shoulder. He flicked off the engine and turned a little in his seat, facing her. "About a year ago I was diagnosed with something called sensorineural hearing loss. It's irreversible and there's no cure. So, I sold my business and moved back to Cedar River."

"Will you lose all your hearing?" she asked. Sean heard her carefully pronounce every word and then tensed because that was exactly what he *didn't* want to happen.

"Possibly," he replied. "It could get to a certain point and plateau. Like, at the moment I can hear you fine because we're sitting in this car and there's no background noise. Sometimes I can hear a sound but not quite work out what it is—like a bird chirping. Conversations can be difficult if I'm with more than one person and everyone is talking at the same time. Crowded bars and restaurants. Stadiums. When I can control my suroundings, like when I'm watching television, I can move the volume up or down as needed. I guess I'm learning as I go along."

She was silent for a moment—which he liked—but he knew it meant she was cultivating more nosy questions. And he wasn't disappointed. "Do you need a hearing aid?"

"It's something that needs consideration."

"What do you mean, consideration?" she asked. "I mean, if it helps, why not do it sooner rather than later?"

"Because I…" He stopped, thinking that he didn't

need to explain his motives to anyone, particularly to a woman he hardly knew. "Let's just drop it, okay."

Silence quickly thickened the air between them until she spoke again. Because she didn't drop it.

"Sean... Did you really have to give up your career?"

"Yes," he said quickly and then shook his head. "No. I don't know. I was pissed off. Mad at myself and the world and all I could think was that a music producer isn't much use if he can't hear the music."

"Maybe with special equipment, you might be able to—"

"To what?" he asked, cutting her off. "Have people feeling sorry for me? Giving me advice? Thinking I was somehow...less, or not as capable. No, thanks."

"Do you really believe people would think that?" she asked slowly.

He raised a brow. "Well, look at it this way, you've known for all of ten seconds and you're already over-enunciating every word you speak. So yeah, I think people might."

"I'm sorry," she said quickly. "I didn't mean to offend you."

"You didn't," he said. "And I didn't mean to bark at you. How about we forget about it and get back to what we were doing?"

She was unusually quiet for the remainder of the drive, and he wondered if she didn't want to deal with the inevitable difficulty of trying to easily communicate. He expected people would get frustrated. In LA, he had a few friends who'd showed the early frustrated signs, even though they didn't know about his diagnosis. It was sure to get worse the more his condition progressed.

"Wow," she said when they finally drove through the gates of the O'Sullivan ranch. Sean had to admit the place was impressive—like one of those spreads in a magazine. White fencing, green pastures, a sprawling house with a wide veranda and timber shutters. "Awesome. I mean, I've seen pictures…but up close it's something else."

He nodded. "It was a good place to grow up."

"Happy?" she asked.

"Mostly," he replied. "Of course, back then we didn't know about my father's double life. Or Jonah. I guess we were happy enough. I remember how Liz and I used to hide under the veranda and spray Mom's ankles with a water pistol."

She smiled. "You and Liz were close?"

He nodded again, his chest tightening as he drove up to the house. "She was six years older than me and always getting me into trouble. But yeah, we were close."

"I can't imagine how it must feel to lose a sibling," she said and sighed. "I mean, after losing my mom, and with Dad's recent stroke, if anything happened to David…" She visibly shuddered. "I couldn't bear it. It's amazing how well your whole family has coped."

"I'm not sure we have," he said flatly. "The truth

is, we don't talk about it much. Kieran will, because he's one of those people who like to talk about things. But Liam's about as closed off as I am, and my dad's not much better. And since I know it upsets Mom to talk about it, I don't. So I guess we're as screwed up as every other family. Except yours," he added. "You and your dad and brother are tight."

"Yeah," she agreed. "But we had our share of loss, just like your family."

Sean pulled up in the driveway and switched off the engine. "It's amazing we both turned out so normal and well-adjusted," he said and grinned in her direction.

She laughed, and the sound reverberated in his chest. "Maybe that's why my dad and your mom have become friends…you know, kindred spirits." She was looking at him. "Like you and me."

"That's right," Sean said and opened the door. "We are going to try the *friends* thing."

"We're off to a pretty good start I think," she said and grabbed her tote before she got out of the car, shut the door and moved around the hood.

"Leah," he said, gently grabbing her hand. "You won't say anthing, will you?"

She frowned. "To your brother? Of course not. You told me in confidence and you have my word I won't betray that."

"Thank you. And you know, when we're this close," he said, rubbing her fingertips with his thumb, "I can hear you just fine."

Color tinged her cheeks. "Okay."

At that moment Sean spotted Kieran striding onto the veranda. "Let's go," he said and released her, ushering her forward and up the steps, where they greeted his brother.

"How's Ivan doing?" Kieran asked as they walked into the house.

"Better," she replied and chuckled. "Complaining about the rehab, of course, but improving every day."

"He's a tough nut, that's for sure," Kieran said and led them down the hall and toward the huge kitchen in the center of house.

"I'm not sure I properly thanked you for looking after him so well when he had his stroke," she said.

"No thanks required," Kieran replied. "Just doing my job."

Sean knew it was more than that. His brother genuinely cared for his patients and was known for his compassionate and caring bedside manner. Sometimes, Sean considered what his brother did for a living and often came out thinking his career was shallow and pointless by comparison. Then he had to remind himself about how many people he'd employed over the years and how many careers he'd help launch. How many people might have been moved by the music he'd helped create.

So yeah, maybe he wasn't saving lives, but in a way he was changing them.

All in the past now though.

"This place is amazing," Leah said and let out a

long and admiring whistle as they passed the wide staircase that led upstairs.

"Mom moved out after the divorce," Kieran stated and sighed. "Too many memories I suppose. She said the house needed a family in it, and she was right. The boys love living here, and Nicola has really helped me make it a home."

As they rounded the corner into the kitchen, Kieran's wife, Nicola, came into view from her position behind the long countertop. "Hi there," she said and smiled, and her gesture broadened when she recognized the woman at his side. "Hello, Leah, lovely to see you again. Hi, Sean."

He wasn't sure how well acquainted Nicola and Leah were, but judging from their smiles they knew one another reasonably well.

He offered a meager greeting just as her two nephews, Johnny and Marco, came bounding into the room. Nicola had asked if it was okay if the kids called him uncle, and he didn't mind. They were nice boys and mostly well behaved. And his brother had taken to fatherhood like a duck to water. Understandable, he supposed, since Kieran had been married once before and had a son—well, a child he'd assumed was his son until his then wife announced that the boy had been fathered by another man. Unhappy times, for sure, but Kieran seemed to have put it all behind him and was clearly very much in love with his new family.

"So, should we get started on this new sound system?" he suggested, and the kids cheered excitedly. Sean glanced in Leah's direction. "Be back soon."

"Sure," she said and perched herself on one of the counter stools.

He smiled a little and left the room, following his brother into the theater room at the rear of the house, once Kieran had gotten the boys out of the way by sending them off, groaning, to clean their rooms. Their father, J.D., had designed the extravagant space several years earlier, incorporating leather recliners in front of a state-of-the-art movie and sound system. He knew the kids did most of their gaming in the room, but Kieran wanted to install a better sound system in their bedrooms.

"So, you and Leah?" Kieran teased.

His brother said something else he didn't catch. "What?"

"I said," Kieran replied, "she's not your usual type."

"She's not my type at all. We're only friends."

"Since when do you have female friends?"

"Since now," he said and grabbed a box filled with electronic equipment that they would be using in the bedrooms.

"If you ask me," Kieran said and grabbed the other box, "it's an improvement."

"I'm not asking," Sean said tersely. "And it's not up for discussion."

"If you bring her here, be prepared for an inquisition. Anyway, I think it will do you good to hang out with Leah. She's nice."

"I know."

Kieran stopped what he was doing and grinned. "You like her."

"What?"

"You *like* her," his brother said again. "As more than a friend."

"No," he said quickly and ignored the tightness in his chest. He didn't want Kieran getting any ideas and then sharing them with Liam and his mom or anyone else.

"You haven't brought a girl home since you were sixteen years old," Kieran reminded him.

That was true. Back then he'd been convinced that Raina Miles was the love of his life. Unfortunately, her parents had moved away at the start of senior year, and he never saw her again. On reflection, he figured that was the last time he'd been in love. Slim pickings, he realized. All the years in LA, all the women who'd shared his bed—none had ever touched his heart.

"I think I'm too selfish to fall in love with someone."

Kieran stopped walking and looked at him. "Scared and selfish are two very different things."

Sean laughed. "I'd hate you to get straight to the point."

"Big brother privileges." Kieran sighed. "The truth is, you don't seem like yourself."

Sean knew his brother's intuition served him well as a doctor—he just didn't want that scrutiny turned on *him*. "I'm fine."

But he knew he couldn't keep up the pretense for much longer.

Leah had met Nicola several times over the years. While not exactly friends, they were friendly and she liked her a lot. But she felt strangely conspicuous in the other woman's kitchen and endured Nicola's scrutiny for about thirty seconds before she spoke.

"Before you ask," Leah said and raised a brow, "your brother-in-law and I are not dating. We are just friends."

Nicola shrugged. "Not my business. Although it's good to see Sean has given up being a hermit."

She smiled. "I don't think the hermit thing suited him all that much."

Nicola laughed. "He's a hottie, isn't he? Undoubtedly the most attractive of the O'Sullivan males."

"And way out of my league," Leah said and chuckled. "If I was, you know, interested."

Nicola's expression widened. "Which of course you're not?"

"Of course," she replied. "That would be ridiculous."

"Sure," Nicola mused. "Only, sometimes it's fun to be a little ridiculous."

Leah laughed and relaxed. Nicola was good company, and for the next half hour they talked about everyday and mundane things—like J.D.'s planned surprise birthday party to the upcoming charity benefit held at O'Sullivan's to aid the museum and art gallery.

"Gwen was telling me about it," she said and sipped the coffee Nicola had made. "I need to convince my brother to sponsor a table—David's got more money than he knows what to do with."

"He was in the same year as Kieran and I in high school. I heard he's getting married again."

She nodded. "Yes, to Annie. She's awesome and the kids adore her."

Nicola shook her head. "It was so sad what happened to his first wife. And of course you both lost your mom as well in the plane crash. But it's lovely that he's met someone else now."

Leah's throat tightened. "I'm very happy for my brother. And Annie's such a good stepmom to his kids. I've always thought it takes someone with an extra-big heart to take on someone else's children. Like you did," she acknowledged gently.

Nicola smiled a little. "We had some tough times in the beginning. Of course the boys miss their parents, and I miss my big brother and sister-in-law. But we've worked hard to make a strong family together."

Leah noticed how Nicola's hand strayed to her belly for a moment, and a tiny smile was etched at one corner of her mouth. But she didn't make any assumptions. Instead, she kept the conversation as general as she could. "Family is the most important

"So, you're a Boy Scout?"

He grinned. "Not exactly. But sometimes it's easier to let people think about you in certain way to avoid people *thinking* about you, if that makes sense."

"Like your mother," she suggested. "Who thinks it would be good for you to settle down, have a couple of kids and a picket fence life?"

"She's my mom," he agreed, "so she's wired to think that way. And she's probably right. I just don't think *I'm* wired that way. The truth is, I've never really done what's been expected of me. I left town, instead of staying to work alongside my father in the family business. I left college after two semesters and then followed my gut, building the career I wanted, on my own terms. I'm the clichéd black sheep."

"A black sheep's wool is warmer," she offered [f]olishly, feeling as though she'd somehow found a [ki]ndred spirit in Sean, and liked the feeling because [sh]e'd also spent most of her life feeling as though [she] didn't quite belong.

["I] don't think that's true."

[H]e shrugged. "It sounds true."

[She] laughed. "Is your glass always half full, [Sean?]"

["No]t usually," she replied. "But since you're so [...] it makes me seem like I believe in rainbows [and unic]orns."

["I'm b]etting you actually do believe in rainbows [and unic]orns," he said and grinned. "And I don't [...] be moody again. It seems to be my fallback."

thing in the world. I know I feel blessed to belong to the one I have, even though we drive each other crazy at times. But when we're all together, you know, all the McCalls and the Petrovics and Culhanes…it feels as though I'm the luckiest person in the world be a part of something so amazing."

Nicola smiled warmly. "I know what you mean. And I know Kieran is happy that Sean's back so he can be a part of things with the family. Everything has mostly smoothed over with Jonah and since J.D. married Kathleen, and well, everyone is trying to get along."

"Everyone except Sean?" she suggested.

Nicola shrugged. "It's been harder for him since he hasn't been living here. Jonah is a good man, and Kieran has worked hard on building a relationship with him. I mean, they're brothers. Sean will realize that in time."

Leah felt an inexplicable urge to defend him. "I'm sure you're right. I guess he's taking things slowly and obviously needs more time to come to terms with all the changes."

It was another twenty minutes before the men returned to the kitchen. Leah's stomach flipped a little when she spotted Sean walking through the doorway, and she had to admit that in chinos, a gray shirt, a leather belt and boots he looked good. Really good. She silently cursed herself for noticing and sipped on the second cup of coffee Nicola had provided.

Friend zone, remember!

And really, she wasn't in any kind of place to think about them being anything other than that, despite the way he made her twitch.

Twitch?

Really...is that what he did?

It had been so long since she'd twitched, itched, craved or longed for a man she could hardly remember. Two years, she thought and grimaced. It was as though she'd put her libido on ice since Xavier had swooped in and stolen her money, her heart *and* her trust.

But...lately she started to thaw.

Don't be an idiot over a man...not again.

She thought about what Sean had told her and wondered how significant his hearing loss was. He was clearly uncomfortable talking about it, and she understood his reluctance. Sean was a private person, and they hardly knew one another. Which made her wonder why he'd told her in the first place. Her brother often said she had a way of getting people to open up. Perhaps she came across as trusting and approachable. She certainly had her own complicated history of being trusting and gullible.

"Ready to go?" he asked, looking a little twitchy himself.

Leah slid off the stool. "Sure."

Once they'd said their goodbyes she followed him outside, and they were quickly on their way back toward Cedar River. He didn't say anything for a while, and she was happy to look out the window and ad-

mire the scenery. When they hit the main road to town, Leah let out a long sigh.

"Did you say something?" he asked.

"No," she replied, but her curiosity piqued. "Do you need me to talk louder?"

"Not exactly," he returned. "Just speak clearly and don't whisper. And I will probably ask you to repeat yourself if I need to."

"No problem," she said. "Thanks for letting me know. Do you need to get your car modified?" she asked, looking at the dash.

"Well, I haven't so far," he replied. "If I ne I will."

She nodded. "Your brother and sister-in really nice people. I'll always be grateful for helping my dad when he was sick."

"He's a good doctor. And a good ma quietly, and then his tone altered and "I wonder what it's like…"

Leah stared at him. "What what"

He shrugged. "Living such a va ing people. Being the best versio

"Don't you believe you are?"

"Not consistently," he repli are elements of my life that perficial."

"Like the red sports ca

He chuckled humorles car isn't a big deal in L frequent as my reputa

"Isn't that partly why we've agreed to be friends, to get you out of your funk?"

"Actually, it was to stop my mother from matchmaking," he replied and drove the car across the bridge and turned left onto Main Street.

"Because I'm not your type."

"And I'm not yours," he reminded her. "Which is why we make perfect friends. There's no...tension."

His words, although she was certain were not meant to offend, made her feel about as desirable as a sack of potatoes. Because he *was* her type. She absolutely, 100 percent, was attracted to Sean and wanted to jump his bones. Of course she would never, ever, show it. And never tell a soul. Even when she was having drinks with her cousin Ellie and friend Winona the night before, and they'd teased her about crushing on him, she'd categorically denied it and assured them that they were just friends. And, of course she was lying through her teeth. But since she'd made such a fool of herself over Xavier, she had no intention of admitting she was hot for someone who had the same lethal combo of looks and sexiness.

"Yeah," she agreed, cringing inwardly. "No blip. No pressure."

"It's a nice change. I like hanging out with you."

She liked it, too. "Want to grab coffee and a doughnut before we head to the hardware store?"

He nodded and turned the car toward the bakery. They stopped for about ten minutes, snacked on chocolate croissants and got their coffee to go and were at the hardware store before midday. Since he appeared to never have been in the place before, Leah urged him toward the paint section.

"This way," she said and grabbed his hand.

And then wished she hadn't, because his touch was electric and sent a bolt of something—she wasn't sure what—race up her arm, which then made her skin scorch and her blood pressure sky rocket, and she groaned before she had a chance to stop herself.

"You okay?" he asked.

She nodded and discreetly tried to remove her hand, but his fingers were now around hers and he didn't appear to be in any hurry to release her. She met his gaze, feeling the heat coming off him, and thinking that in someplace called *Leah's Stupid Fantasies*, she saw something in his expression that was definitely outside the friend zone.

He's not attracted to you, remember?
He's mentioned the fact several times.
Don't be an idiot.

Leah swallowed hard and pointed to the paint color swatches, ignoring the heat in her arm, her chest and her legs. "Pick a color."

He moved a little closer, and she inhaled the woodsy cologne he wore, which was instantly like catnip for her sex-starved pheromones. She shuddered out a breath, trying not to think about how he still held her hand and was standing ridiculously close.

"You pick," he said.

Leah stared at him, suddenly outraged—not only by her surging libido, but by his very obvious indifference to their close proximity. "It's your house."

"And you're the artist," he reminded her. "I trust your instincts."

He wouldn't trust her so much if he suspected she was itching to plant a kiss on his perfectly sinful throat. "What's your favorite color?"

"Blue," he replied.

She nodded and scanned the swatches, acutely conscious that he was still holding her hand, but didn't want to be obvious and pull away first because then he might suspect what she was thinking. "This one," she said and pulled out a card that showed a pale blue named after some cool arctic reference.

He looked at the swatch and nodded. "Sure."

"And you need brushes and rollers and stuff, right?"

"I guess."

She rolled her eyes. "Have you ever painted a room before?"

"No," he replied, not looking the faintest bit embarrassed. "If I wanted something done, I paid a contractor to do it."

"City boy," she teased and then met his gaze. "Ah...my hand?"

He glanced to where their fingers were linked and quickly released her. "Sorry."

Leah managed a casual shrug and tried to ignore

the tingling that remained after his touch ended. *Stupid. Foolish. Fantasy.* She said the words over and over to herself like a chant as she walked on ahead and perused the brushes and equipment needed. After a couple of minutes, she made a selection and instructed him to hold out his arms, which she filled with several items.

"That should do it," she said and hauled a couple of plastic tarps off the rack. "I'll see if we can get this stuff delivered this afternoon." She headed toward the front counter.

She knew the elderly sales clerk, Morris, as he was a friend of her father's. "Hey, Morris," she greeted as they approached the desk. "Any chance you could get your grandson to deliver these to Spruce Road this afternoon?" she asked and gave the exact address.

The older man gave Sean a quick once-over and then nodded. "Anything for you, sweet thing. How's your dad feelin'?"

"Much better. I've moved in for a while, so I can keep a close eye on him," she said and winked.

The older man nodded. "And who's this?" he asked and gestured in Sean's direction. She quickly made the introductions. "Don't I feel fancy," Morris teased, laughing loudly. "We don't usually get the O'Sullivans in the store. The hotel gets me to deliver their supplies. If I'd known you were coming, I would have pulled out the good china and red carpet."

She could feel Sean tense for a second and she quickly grabbed his arm, squeezing the hard muscle and almost groaning at how good it felt. She released him abruptly and allowed him to place the items on the counter and then pay for them.

"Thank you," he said and took the receipt.

Leah chatted to Morris for another few moments and then left the store, Sean striding at her side. Once they were back in the car, she spoke. "You look pissed."

His mouth curled at her words, and she wasn't about to admit that she had something of a potty mouth. Then he laughed humorlessly. "The O'Sullivan reputation reaches far and wide, I see."

"He was only teasing. And well, your dad and Liam aren't exactly the handyman type who frequent hardware stores, are they?" she remarked and grinned.

"There's that rich and entitled stereotype again."

"If the stereotype fits," she teased and laughed.

His scowl slowly disappeared. "I don't think I've ever known a woman quite like you, Leah."

Her brows rose for dramatic effect. "You mean one who doesn't pander your giant ego?"

"Precisely."

She laughed. "That will never be me."

He didn't offer a reply, and Leah relaxed in the seat. Once they were heading back across the bridge and toward the river, he spoke again.

"Leah, what are you doing next Sunday?"

She turned her head. "Ah…why?"

"I have this thing," he said, a little uneasily. "My

dad's surprise birthday party, and I was wondering…" He paused, looking directly ahead, fingers tight on the steering wheel. "Ah…would you like to come with me?"

It sounded like a date. But since he wasn't into her in that way, she didn't dare allow herself the fantasy. Most likely he wanted a gal pal to hang out with so his mother and siblings would get off his back about remaining resolutely single.

The thing was, she also needed her own date for Annie and David's wedding in five days. Which gave her an idea.

"Sure," she said quickly. "If you come as my plus-one to my brother's wedding on Saturday."

He grinned. "It's a deal."

Chapter Six

Sean had no real desire to go to Leah's brother's wedding. But since he also didn't want to go stag to his own family shindig, helping each other out seemed like the perfect solution.

Once they were back at his house, he opened the automatic garage door and drove the car inside. She got out and walked outside, letting out a long and appreciative whistle.

"I really think this is one of the best spots along the river," she said and pointed to a bend along the riverbank. "That's my cousin Jake's place."

"Liam lives next door to him," he stated. "Biggest block in the area, of course. My brother always has to have the best."

Leah raised her brows and looked at him, jerking a thumb in the direction of the garage. "He's not the one driving the Ferrari though, is he?"

"Damn, you're hard on me," he said and grinned. "Want a tour of the place?"

"No need," she replied. "I've been here before. I looked at it when it came on the market. Back before my ex stole my money."

"You planned on buying it?" he asked quietly.

She shrugged. "Maybe. It's all moot now. I'm broke and it belongs to you."

Guilt stupidly pressed down on his shoulders. "I'm sorry."

"You couldn't know," she said and stood in front of him. "A car's coming. Must be the hardware store."

True enough, a pickup came barreling down the driveway and a young man with scruffy red hair dropped off the paint and equipment. Leah chatted to the youth for a few minutes while Sean took the equipment into the house. He waited for her to head inside and quickly met her by the front door. She walked through the house and nodded appreciatively.

"It looks great in here. Did you have your furniture hauled from LA?"

"Nope," he replied. "I hired a decorator to style the place. You know me," he added when she gave him a questionable look. "Besides, decorating isn't my thing. Making coffee, though, is something I'm very good at."

She chuckled and followed him into the kitchen. "Can you cook?"

"Actually...yes," he admitted. "It's another thing I'm good at. I'll cook you dinner sometime. I make an awesome linguini."

"So many talents," she teased. "What else are you good at?"

"Making coffee. Poker," he said and cranked up the coffee machine. "And Scrabble."

She perched on a counter stool and smiled. "Anything else?"

Sean's mouth curled at the edges. "Sex."

She stilled for a moment and then chuckled. "What about kissing? That's way more important than sex."

He tried to ignore the heat suddenly surging through his blood and grabbed a couple of mugs, facing her across the countertop. "I haven't had any complaints," he replied and smiled a little more.

Sean watched as she bit down on her lower lip, and it highlighted the lushness of her mouth and the vibrancy of her green eyes. Somehow it managed to increase the heat swirling in his gut. If he'd expected her to be embarrassed by his mild flirting, he was wrong. She didn't look the least bit undone. Leah could hold her own, that was for sure.

"You're a confident guy," she remarked and rested her elbows on the counter.

He shrugged shamelessly. "Perhaps I should say, not that I know of."

Her brows arched dramatically. "Do you think kissing is important?"

"Absolutely."

"Me, too," she said and grinned.

"Sugar?" he asked.

She shook her head. "On reflection, my last boy-friend Xavier was a terrible kisser."

"Was he?" he queried, not liking the way the idea of her kissing someone else made him feel. He'd never been the jealous type. Jealousy meant feelings. And having feelings beyond friendship for Leah was out of the question.

"Oh," she added and waved a hand, "not techni-cally… I mean, he knew what he was doing…but he always treated it like it was a means to an end, if you get what I mean."

"He was more interested in the finish line?"

She nodded. "Yeah…as though it was a race. But I like kissing. I could do it for hours. Not that I ever have," she said, then grinned and rested her chin on her hands. "But it would be fun, I think, just to kiss someone for the simple pleasure of it. Without an agenda. Or end game in mind."

Sean's collar felt uncomfortably tight, but he mustered all his self-control and ignored it, as well as the way his awareness of her had suddenly shifted on some weird axis. All he could do was stare at her mouth and imagine what it would be like to kiss her.

Over and over.

All over…

"I guess it's the whole idea of men and women thinking about sex differently," he added hurriedly.

She nodded. "Yeah, no doubt. I think it must feel different when we actually make love, as opposed to simply having sex. You know, to be with someone and it's more than physical, more than just a few seconds of orgasmic bliss. When the touching is so intense you can't bear it if it stops. Or when you can be side by side and look into each other's eyes and know that they're the only person's eyes you want to see your own reflection in."

She stopped and sighed heavily, her cheeks redder than usual, her green eyes darker, her lovely mouth fuller, her gaze completely focused on him, and the moment was intensely erotic. He wondered if she knew how sexy she was, if she was aware that her skin flushed with a rosy hue when she spoke. But no...there was nothing overt or deliberate about Leah. She was all color and creative passion...an artist, an old soul, someone who put all of herself into everything she did and every word she spoke. And he remembered how he'd tried to convince himself she wasn't attractive and admitted he'd been kidding himself. Because there was something about her that got his attention. Something that made him want to spend time with her. Something he couldn't define. He wondered, not as vaguely as he probably should have, if her skin flushed that same rosy hue in places that never saw the sun...

"So, do I need to wear a suit to this wedding?"

Sean asked, trying to shift his thoughts away from her skin, her mouth and every other part of her.

"Yes," she replied. "Do you have one?"

"Armani," he replied, referring to a comment she'd previously made about her slick, city-boy ex. "The party is also fairly formal."

"I'll frock up accordingly," she said and grinned. "Shall we start painting?"

Sean nodded. Although the last thing he wanted to do was paint. What he actually wanted to do was stride around the counter, haul her into his arms and kiss her like crazy.

No. Chance. In. Hell.

"Sure thing," he said and quickly shook off the idea.

Three days after their painting endeavors, Sean dropped by her father's house for dinner. Now that she was settled into her dad's place and into her old room, Leah knew she'd done the right thing by moving back in. She liked that she could discreetly manage her father's physio appointments and ensure he was eating well and doing his exercises.

Dinner was her way of being neighborly, since she appreciated the time Sean spent playing chess with her dad. She suspected that Sean liked their quiet, nonquestioning camaraderie. Since her dad also liked long silences and solitude, chess was the perfect pastime for both men.

"Thank you for being Dad's friend."

Sean looked up from the dinner table. The meal was done, and Ivan had retired to the living room to watch a show on the History Channel. Leah was clearing plates when she spoke.

"What?" he asked, a little frustrated. "Don't turn your back on me," he said tightly, getting to his feet and touching her shoulder.

She turned to face him, awareness coming into her expression. "I'm sorry. I should have realized you couldn't follow what I was saying with my back to you. I was thanking you for being such a good friend to my dad." She hesitated. "The truth is, Sean… I'd like to better understand what you're feeling and how I can… I don't know. Help."

Sean sighed heavily. "No… I'm sorry. I didn't mean to snap at you. I just have things on my mind."

"What things?" she asked, meeting his gaze, thinking that she really did need to stop imagining there was more between them than friendship, even though they'd seen one another every day since Saturday. "Tell me."

He sighed again. "I have an appointment on Tuesday with an audiologist in Rapid City, a referral from my doctor in LA. I think the whole thing is making me…you know…"

"Grumpier than usual?" she teased and then smiled. "It's perfectly natural. I'm sure it will be fine."

"I'm going deaf," he reminded her. "My life *is* going to change."

She reached out and touched his forearm. "It'll be okay, Sean," she offered, meaning it, but knowing it was an inadequate response. "I know I can't understand exactly what you're feeling, but I do believe that when you're ready, you will find a way to navigate through this."

He nodded. "I guess I wasn't expecting this kind of change."

"You're grieving," she said gently. "You know, missing what you used to have…your old life."

"Maybe," he said and grabbed the empty breadbasket from the table and a couple of plates before he walked around the counter. "But the truth is, I don't really miss that life. At least not the parts that now seem superficial. I miss working," he admitted. "I miss being a part of something. I miss contributing to something. I miss working with people who are just starting out—those artists who have big dreams and just need someone to believe in them. You know, I've got more money than I know what to do with. A nice house. A fancy car. And no idea what I'm going to do with the rest of my life." He made a self-disgusted sound. "Poor me, right?"

Leah touched his arm, feeling the tension like it had a life force of its own. "Despair is a normal human reaction. So is fear, and confusion. But you'll get through it. You're a talented guy who knows how to be successful. Look at everything you've accomplished. I know you can work through this, too."

He placed a hand over hers and squeezed her fingers softly. "Thanks for the vote of confidence. And you're right... I just need to figure out what I want to do. What about you?" he asked, and was suddenly stroking her knuckles with his thumb. "What do you want?"

Leah swallowed hard. "I want... I want to be happy."

"And what makes you happy?"

"Sculpting, painting, working in my studio. Being with my family. My friends. My dogs."

His mouth curled at the edges. "That's a lot of things. You're lucky."

"I feel lucky," she said honestly. "For a long time though, I didn't. After Gary, after Xavier..." Her voice trailed off, and she was hypnotized by the feel of his thumb brushing across her skin. "After my mom died...all I felt was alone. But time is a good healer. And when one person leaves your life, sometimes, if you're lucky, someone else comes into it."

"Your optimism is something I like about you, Leah. It's very...comforting."

"I think that's one of the nicest things anyone has ever said to me."

"I can be nice," he said, still touching her, still working his own brand of magic on her skin, her thoughts and her awakening libido. Even if she could never acknowledge it. Never admit to him that in the past week she'd begun to feel inexplicably drawn toward him. Because he didn't feel that way about her, and she wasn't about to start imagining anything different.

"I'm sure you can," she said and pulled back, putting space between them. "So, what kind of new career are you thinking about? You know, maybe music isn't as lost to you as you think. There have to be other things in the industry you can do that are just as satisfying."

He nodded and dropped his hand. "Maybe. I've certainly never been interested in the family business."

Leah understood. Sean was a man used to making his own way and not relying on his family. "Maybe you should write a book," she suggested. "I'll bet you have some interesting behind-the-scenes tales from all your time in LA."

He laughed. "Some. But nothing I can write without the prospect of being chased by lawyers for the next ten years. By the way," he added and grabbed the keys and cell phone he'd left on the counter, "it's my pleasure."

Leah stilled. "What is?"

"Being your dad's friend," he replied. "And yours. Anyway, I gotta bail. See you Saturday, if not before."

Leah watched him leave and experienced a familiar sense of solitude once she was alone. She'd become accustomed to her own company in the past few months and was mostly okay with it. But hanging out with Sean had made her think about how much she liked *male* company. And his company in particular. She'd missed it. She missed the warm sound of a man's laughter. She missed the camaraderie, the conversation.

And she missed sex.

Not that Gary or Xavier had been dynamos in bed. And she suspected she wasn't, either. Xavier had called her boring and predictable. Gary said she was afraid to take a chance. But she missed the closeness, the intimacy. Spending time with Sean had amplified how alone she was. And since her brother and Annie got together, she'd come to believe that soul mates were a possibility. Like her mom and dad.

"What did you say, sweetie?"

Leah looked up and spotted her father standing in the doorway. "Nothing. I think I sighed."

Ivan smiled. "Sean's gone home?"

She nodded. "Yep. Well, I think I'll turn in for the night."

"He's spending a lot of time here lately," Ivan mentioned as he came into the room and placed an empty mug in the sink. "And not just to play chess."

Heat climbed up her neck. "We're just hanging out. Don't read anything else into it, Dad."

Ivan shrugged. "Has he told you what's troubling him? I know Gwen is worried."

"Ah...no," she lied, careful not to betray Sean's confidence. "I'm sure it's nothing to worry about."

"Gwen says he's not talking," Ivan said and sighed heavily. "I thought maybe he might have opened up to you. People usually do," he added and kissed her forehead gently. "Good night, hon."

Leah headed for her room and had a quick shower. Afterward, she changed into warm pajamas and settled herself in bed with her tablet and read a book for half an hour. She turned out the light around ten thirty but had an unusually restless night and roused around seven o'clock feeling lethargic and irritable. She spent most of the morning in her workshop, finishing off the piece for the O'Sullivan Hotel foyer, and headed into town around lunchtime to buy a dress for the fancy O'Sullivan birthday party she was attending on Sunday. She met Ellie, Winona and Annie for lunch at the bakery, talked a little about the wedding and any last-minute jobs that needed doing, and then informed her future sister-in-law that she was bringing a date to the wedding.

"I can't believe you're dating an O'Sullivan," Ellie said and frowned a little. "And especially Sean, since he's got the worst reputation when it comes to women."

"I'm pretty sure that most of that talk is simple gossip, considering he has been living in Los Angeles for the past decade," Leah said in defense of Sean and sipped her coffee. "And we're not dating. We're friends. Anyhow, I have to run. I'll see you all on Saturday."

She left the bakery and walked half a block to the hotel, asking the concierge if Liam or the assistant manager, Connie, was available. Liam appeared about five minutes later, and she told him she'd have the piece for the foyer delivered the following morning.

"Great," he said and walked to the spot near the front window. "I'm sure it will look good. My mother has assured me it's a solid investment."

"I hope so. Gwen is very supportive."

"She has an eye for talent. And other things," he added and winked. "I hear you're coming to the party on Sunday?"

"Is that okay?"

"Of course," he replied. "I actually wasn't sure if Sean would show up. But knowing he's bringing you is quite the assurance. So, thank you, for whatever it is that you are doing. He's obviously going through something at the moment. Not that he's talking to me or Kieran about whatever it is, but we appreciate the fact you're in his life."

It sounded absurdly intimate. "I'm not," she insisted. "We're just friends."

He shrugged. "Sometimes that's enough. And it's obviously what he needs. Anyway, I'm looking forward to seeing the sculpture."

Leah said goodbye and headed out, walking toward the museum and art gallery. Liam's wife, Kayla, was the curator, but since the birth of their second child, she worked only part-time. There was an older woman named Shirley who managed the small gift shop and entrance, and she greeted Leah with a warm smile. Leah walked around the gallery for a while, finding comfort among the quiet and solitude. As a teen, troubled by not quite fitting in at school because she was artistic and liked her own company, she'd spent a lot of time in the gallery, sitting by her favorite pieces, imagining that one day she would carve her own career as a successful artist.

No such luck...

She sighed, thinking about her old dreams and her current reality. One piece for the hotel foyer did not make a career. Not that she wasn't grateful to Gwen and Liam for giving her the opportunity. But she knew it wasn't enough. She needed to push past her polarizing insecurity—the thing was, she didn't know how.

"Leah?"

She turned and discovered Sean standing a few feet away from her. "Oh, hi. What are doing here?"

He stepped closer. A habit she'd come to recognize and one she knew had to do with his condition. "I was across the street at the dry cleaner's and saw you."

She nodded. "I was just checking things out. I haven't been here for a while."

He looked around and grinned a little. "Yeah, I have to admit I don't hang out here often."

"Not your scene," she said and relaxed. "I get it."

"It's your scene, though," he said and walked toward a carved timber sculpture in the center of the room. "What's this meant to be?" he asked.

Leah moved beside him and looked over the piece. "I think it's a man and a woman embracing."

He tilted his head, his expression curious and questioning. "Nah...can't see it."

Leah laughed softly. "Look here," she said and traced her hand in an arc along one side of the sculpture. "Here's her waist and hips." She ran her fingers around the wood. "And this is obviously his...butt."

He grinned. "Obviously."

Leah dropped her hand. "Well, that's where I would have put it, if I'd made this piece."

"So," he said and moved toward several more pieces. "Do you have anything on display?"

She shook her head and met his gaze "No. Although..."

"Although?"

"Your mom and Kayla keep asking me to have a showing."

"Why don't you?" he asked bluntly.

Leah sighed. "Oh, you know, blatant insecurity, fear of being humiliated, what if no one turns up... all of the above."

He didn't flinch. "Do you have enough pieces completed for a showing?"

She half shrugged. "Probably. Yes. Sure."

Another couple came into the gallery, and they offered a brief greeting before Sean moved close beside her and led her into the adjoining room, one filled with glass cabinets that housed an array of local indigenous art pieces.

"Then maybe it's worth thinking about."

She looked at him, dropping her guard entirely. "I'm scared, Sean."

"Of what?" he asked gently, tipping his head so close to hers she could feel the heat emanating from him.

"Failing," she admitted. "Proving that the last time I had a showing it was just bad organizing on my manager's part. Of not being good enough. Take your pick."

"Fear is normal. So is insecurity."

"Are you saying that from personal experience?" she asked pointedly.

He smirked. "Absolutely. Remember, Leah, you know all my secrets. So, taking my own foolish pride and fear out of this conversation, the trick, at least as far as I believe, is having people around you who support you and believe in you. Like your dad, and my mother," he said and nodded. "And me. If you want to have a showing, then you should do exactly that."

Leah inhaled a long and shuddering breath. "I wouldn't know where to begin. Or who to invite."

"I'll help you with the arrangements," he said unexpectedly. "I've thrown a shindig or two in the past. And I can work with you on the invitation list."

"I'm not sure I can do—"

"Sure you can," he corrected and smiled. "Trust me."

"I don't trust easily," she admitted. "Not after Gary and Xavier."

"Understandable. But if you don't follow your dreams, then they win, yes?"

Of course he was right. And his words were exactly what she needed to hear. Only, she hadn't expected to find such and understanding ally in Sean. "Okay... I'll think about it."

He said goodbye and left soon after, although Leah hung around the gallery for another half hour. By the time she returned to her dad's place, it was well after four o'clock. She headed for her workshop and began sorting through several pieces that she'd kept under wraps for way too long. Sean was right... it was time she followed her dreams. Since Xavier... since Gary, she'd buried herself into a hole, continuing with her work, but keeping it tucked away, safe from judgment and potential ridicule. Even the teaching job she'd taken at the technical college had been a safety net. Because she could teach, and not *do*. Ivan's stroke and recuperation had also given her another reason to take a step back, to convince herself she had to think about her parent first and her career second. But the truth was, her dad was doing much better than she'd or the doctors expected, and Leah didn't need to monitor him 24/7.

She rummaged through a few storage crates, finding several pieces she knew were good enough for a showing, and quickly grabbed a notepad and pen, and then began taking inventory of the items she would be able to showcase.

By the time she returned to the house, it was past

six o'clock and her dad was in the kitchen, reheating lasagna. She hung up her coat by the door and fed the dogs and cat.

"What were you doing out there this late?" he asked and passed her the plates across the counter. Ivan never interrupted her when she was in her studio.

"Sorting through some of my finished pieces."

Ivan's silvery brows rose up instantly. "Got something going on?"

She shrugged. "Maybe. I'm in the considering stage."

"What brought this on?"

"Oh, just some honest feedback I received from a friend about how being afraid means I let Gary and Xavier win."

Ivan grabbed cutlery and moved slowly toward the table. "Friend?" he queried.

Leah held out a chair for her father and then sat down. "Oddly," she said and smiled, "Sean and I get along pretty well most of the time. We straight talk each other. It's nice for a change. For the last few years, I've felt as though I've been sheltered from the real world. And I get why," she added, her voice quiet and solemn. "After Mom died, and my two failed relationships, along with my fear of getting my career off the ground… I'm sure that you and David thought I was fragile. And you were right, I was. But I need to get some strength back into my spine and get on with my life. Or at least have the gumption to try."

"I'm proud of you," Ivan said, his eyes glittering. "And grateful to Sean."

Leah's throat tightened. "We'll see what happens. In the meantime, tell me how physical therapy went today?"

They chatted for a while and once Ivan headed for the living room, Leah hung around the kitchen and cleaned up. Ivan, weary from his day, retired early to his room and Leah busied herself in the pantry, rearranging the already neat rows of herbs in jars. It was eight o'clock when her cell pinged and she quickly checked the message.

Lonely? It's a nice night. Feel like hanging out by the jetty and looking at the stars? S

Leah stared at the message for a second, glanced around at her surroundings and considered her plans for the rest of the evening, and then quickly replied.

See you in ten. L

Her cell pinged again a few seconds later.

It's cold. Bring a warm coat.

She grinned and got ready, wrapping herself up in a long fleecy coat over her jeans and sweater, adding a knitted hat before she slipped on socks and boots. She left a short note for her dad and placed it on the kitchen counter, in case he awoke and wondered about her whereabouts, and then headed outside. The dogs followed, of course, and she was glad for their company as she took the track that led toward Sean's house. She made her way toward the jetty when she spotted a lamplight. He was waiting, with two chairs set out, a couple of lanterns set around and she noticed a bottle of wine and glasses. And he was right—it was a beautiful night. Chilly, but the water glittered in the moonlight, and the sky was clear and filled with stars.

"This was a good idea," she said as the dogs greeted him. He didn't respond, and she figured he hadn't heard her over the night noise that surrounded them. She spoke again, louder and clearer, and this time he replied.

"Seemed a shame to waste a night like this sitting around indoors."

"The air is so clear here," she said as she inhaled and took a seat, smiling as the dogs curled around his jean-clad legs. "They like you."

He petted both hounds and they relaxed and lay down by his chair. "Well, I am very charming."

Leah laughed and accepted a glass of wine. "And humble."

He chuckled and sat down. The lamps were between them and their chairs almost faced one another, and Leah suspected he'd placed them that way so he could watch her as she spoke.

"What are you thinking?" he asked.

She sighed. "That I know you don't like talking about it, but at some point, you're going to have to tell your family. Or at least your mom. Gwen's worried about you. And so is Liam, for that matter. And I get it," she said, speaking again before he could respond. "You don't want pity. But they love you and they're your family, Sean. Don't shut them out."

"My family?" he echoed, his voice oddly cynical. "To be honest, most of the time I feel like I don't belong to them, or them to me."

She nodded, feeling his words through to her bones. "I understand. Some days I feel the same about my own."

He looked surprised. "You do?"

"Sure," she replied and shrugged. "My mom was a Culhane, one of the oldest families in the county. She married a McCall, another well-respected family. When James McCall died, my brother David was only a toddler. And then, a few years later, she up and marries a much older, first-generation American-Slovenian history teacher with no extended family, and no real ties to Cedar River other than the fact he taught at the local high school."

"And that makes you feel like you don't belong?" he asked.

She nodded. "Sometimes I feel like an outsider, as though I'm one of the lesser Culhanes. Not like

David, who's both a Culhane *and* a McCall. Silly, I suppose. And I suspect my Culhane cousins and my brother, David, would be stunned if they knew how I felt. Don't get me wrong. I adore my dad and am so proud to be his daughter and don't need to remind myself how lucky I am to have so many people who love me."

He looked like he understood exactly. "You're right, of course. I know I have to tell them." He paused, watching her over the rim of his glass. "You know, Leah, you are quickly becoming the best friend I've ever had."

Strangely, Leah felt that, too. Sure, she'd made several friends over the course of her life. Like Annie, who was soon to be her sister-in-law, and she was close to Ellie and Winona. But she'd never truly had a *best* friend. Not even in school. Because she was so happy with her own company and spent so much time working on her art, she'd often faced time alone, on the outside of the popular groups in the schoolyard. Not that she was ever bullied or deliberately ostracized, but solitude was often her companion.

"I've never been great at making friends," she admitted.

"Me, either," he said. "My brothers were a hard act to follow in high school. Liam was a football superstar and Kieran was Mr. Popularity. I was the one stuck in my room, dreaming big, teaching myself chords on my guitar and trying to write music."

"I didn't know you played the guitar."

He nodded. "And piano."

"Would you play for me sometime?"

"Sure. But I'm a little out of practice so don't be too critical," he said and chuckled.

"I won't, I promise," she said gently. "Do you still write music?"

"A little. I can feel the shifts in the music using amps. I've been working on my mojo this week," he said and grinned. "You know, trying to figure out what I want to do with the rest of my life."

"Have you made any decisions?"

"Nothing specific," he replied. "But hanging out with you seems to give things more clarity."

"I know what you mean."

Sean looked at her, and she was quickly caught up in his intense stare. He raised his glass and spoke softly. "Here's to misfits. And to friendship."

Leah lifted her glass in a toast, repeating his words, but deep down she was feeling something else. Friendship, certainly. But it was wrapped in something that she'd been denying to herself for the last couple of weeks. Because she liked him. As much more than a friend.

And she knew it was heartbreak in the making.

Chapter Seven

Sean had never liked weddings.

He'd been to more than his fair share during his years in LA. Some were rushed and low-key to avoid paparazzi; some were ridiculously outrageous Hollywood-style events that took place over entire weekends.

This one, though, was peaceful and stylish and very much a family affair. The bride and groom were clearly in love. Surprisingly, he knew several people in attendance and didn't feel like the interloper he'd imagined he'd be. True, he hadn't been surrounded by so many Culhanes since high school, but he didn't feel uncomfortable. And when he'd spotted Jonah amongst the guests, Sean expected his usual resentment to set in. But surprisingly, he was almost relieved to have another O'Sullivan in attendance.

The noise level was manageable, since the band was a soft rock country ensemble. Overall, there were only about fifty or so people gathered under the large tent, and he wasn't straining to hear every word. And since he was seated at a table with Ivan and a couple of the Culhane brothers, Joss and Grant, with Jonah flanking his left side, he managed to make conversation and avoid anyone repeating themselves for his benefit.

"My wife would have loved this," Ivan said, his expression a little sober. "Sandra adored weddings. We had a small wedding, of course, because she was a widow and didn't want to make a fuss. But I'll never forget how lovely she looked. She was such a beauty. Not sure what she saw in me," he added and shrugged. "Just a high school teacher."

"A good man, I suspect," Sean suggested.

"I hope so. I'd like to think I've led a valuable life. Like us all, I suppose." Ivan gestured to the bride and groom and smiled. "They look happy. The kids are flourishing with Annie, and David is such a good father."

Sean nodded. "Well, you raised him, so it's not surprising."

Ivan's eyes glittered. "That's kind. I know he didn't take my name, but I couldn't be prouder to call him my son." He sipped at his club soda. "Do you see much of your father?"

It wasn't exactly a seamless segue, and although he wasn't eager to talk about his own family, he respected Ivan too much to dismiss the question. "Not really," he replied, thinking about how he'd mostly avoided his dad since he'd returned to Cedar River. "It's complicated."

"Family usually is," Ivan remarked. "One thing I've learned over the years is to make the most of every relationship that matters."

"That's good advice. You should take it."

It was Jonah who spoke. Jonah who was weighing in on their conversation.

The thing was, Sean had always had a decent relationship with J.D.—not as good as Liam, but he respected his father and had tried to maintain a connection during the years he was in California. But since he'd come back, things were different. Irrationally, he blamed his half brother. Even though he knew Jonah and J.D.'s relationship had been fractious and difficult over the years, now they seemed to have become pretty tight. And since J.D. had married Jonah's mom, Kathleen, it was harder to breach the divide Sean knew was fueled by his own resentment and disappointment in his father's past behavior.

But he knew he had to try. He'd made the decision to return to Cedar River to get on with his life, and reconnecting with his family was an important part of that. As was getting over his resentment toward Jonah. Logically, he knew Jonah wasn't to blame for J.D.'s infidelity and for his parents' ultimate divorce.

"I'll try," he promised and grinned toward his half brother. "I mean, if you can do it…"

Jonah raised both brows. "That almost sounds like a compliment."

"I wouldn't go that far," Sean replied and then his attention was diverted when he spotted Leah standing by the bridal table, talking with two of the other bridesmaids, one hand on her hip, the other flapping around as she laughed at something one of the other women said. There was something about her posture, about the way she held herself that caught his attention. In a dark purple dress with matching wrap, she looked effortlessly lovely. The color suited her, adding vibrancy to her skin and her fabulous hair. She was truly stunning.

As though she somehow sensed his attention, she turned her head and looked in his direction. Sean smiled, hitching up one brow a little, and within seconds she walked across the space dividing them. When she reached their table, she greeted everyone with a warm smile and it was as though people settled when she was around. He wondered why he hadn't noticed that before, or how he hadn't realized that she had a soothing effect on others. It seemed at odds with the way she often described herself, as sort of a quirky loner who didn't have many friends.

She moved around the table and stood between Sean and her father, resting a soft hand on Sean's shoulder. Somehow, it seemed absurdly intimate. But since he'd arrived as her date, obviously people would assume there was more intimacy to their relationship than there actually was.

She leaned down close, her mouth close to his ear, her breath warm on his neck. "Wanna dance, Hollywood?"

Sean smirked. "Hollywood?"

He felt her smile against his earlobe. "I promise I won't tell anyone I called you that."

Sean grasped her hand, swiveled in his seat and stood, excusing them both. He saw Ivan grinning and figured the older man was suspicious something more was going on with them. But it wasn't. She was his friend. That was it. They weren't lovers.

Not yet...

Sean shook the thought off as he led her to the dance floor. Thinking about Leah in that way was out of the question. But still, he mused as he gathered her close and curved one arm around her waist and settled a hand on her hip, she felt good in his arms. Almost like...

She belonged there.

Don't be an idiot.

He knew what it was. He'd been alone too long. He was lonely and horny and that was it—and since Leah was the only woman in his sphere, his libido had gone into a red alert when she was so close. Natural, he thought and endeavored to shrug off the idea.

He'd never been a fan of country music, but the band was a good one and their covers respectable. As they swayed together, she leaned in closer, her breasts pressing against him lightly and he fought the urge to pull away—and the other urge, this one stronger and more resilient, to move in and feel all of her against him. Guilt pressed down on his shoulders, and he mentally tried to talk himself out of thinking she felt good, or how the fragrance she wore seemed to circle around him like a cloak. Or how her hand felt resting against his shoulder, or that the way her thighs would occasionally brush against him as they moved together warmed his blood and made him think about how great it would feel to kiss the sweet curve of her neck, or stroke his fingertips along her spine.

Don't think about sex. Don't think about sex. Don't think about sex...

"What are you thinking about?" she asked, leaning in and moving closer so she could speak into his ear.

"Sex," he said baldly and immediately wished he hadn't.

She pulled back a little and met his gaze. "Oh... okay."

"Don't freak out," he said when he saw the way her luscious mouth tightened. "I was just...thinking."

"And flirting?"

He grinned. "Maybe a little. It's a wedding, after all."

She nodded, still dancing, although he was sure that her hips were swaying a little more. "And hookups are inevitable, right? Unfortunately for you, I don't see any leggy blondes here tonight."

"Actually, I was thinking more about brunettes," he said, taking the flirting up a notch. "And one brunette in particular."

Her fingers curled into his shoulder. "Really?"

He nodded. "Really."

"Even though I'm not your type?" she remarked, staring at him, eyes wide.

Sean inched closer, moving his hand a little on her hip. "Well, things seemed to have changed there."

She snorted softly. "Are we talking a sort of friends with benefits kind of thing?"

He cringed. "I guess…not that I've ever had one of those."

"Me, either," she admitted.

"It might be fun."

She nodded, but looked a little more serious. "There are risks."

"Such as?" he asked, linking their fingers intimately.

She sighed. "Oh, you know, the usual…potentially falling in love, potentially falling out of love and definitely ending up hating each other."

"Then we won't," he returned, urging her closer until there wasn't any space between them. "Fall in love. I'm not the fall in love type, anyway, so you're safe."

As he said the words, his gut twitched. Deep down, Sean knew his inability to truly get close to someone was his greatest flaw. But he wasn't going to lie to her. He didn't *do* love. He did sex, monogamy, honesty and consideration. But he wasn't looking for a relationship. And pretending he did simply to get her into bed wasn't his style.

"Okay, we won't fall in love," she said. "So, I guess that means you'll be taking me home tonight?"

"Well, we are on a date," he reminded her. "I usually take my dates home. Even if they live next door."

Which meant two things—first, he and Leah *were* going to be lovers. And second—things were about to become a whole lot more complicated.

So, maybe Sean *didn't* fall in love. But she *did*. And although hooking up with him had disaster written all over it, she didn't care.

Leah wasn't sure what had set her mood off. The wedding. The romantic music. The fancy dress she was wearing. Seeing Sean in his suit and having a kind of *lust-at-first-sight* reaction, or the two glasses of wine, or the cake, or a combination of everything that made her swoony and susceptible to male attention. And Sean's attention in particular, because he looked so freaking hot and sexy she just wanted to rip off his clothes and have her way with him at the first opportunity. And now, knowing he wasn't as immune to her as she'd initially believed, her pulses shot upward, *à la* space rocket, and she could barely suck in a breath.

When the song ended, she pulled back and excused herself, saying she needed to get back to the wedding-party table. He smiled, grabbed her hand and pressed a soft kiss to her knuckles before releasing her and returning to his table. Leah immediately felt the loss of his arms around her and cursed her foolishness as she walked back to her own table.

"Just friends, huh?"

It was Ellie, dressed in an identical gown, who'd sidled up beside her and spoke. Leah shrugged. "Yep. Just friends."

"I've got friends," her cousin said and grinned. "And we don't dance like that."

Color crept up her neck. "I don't know…something's changed."

"For him or for you?" Ellie asked.

"Both," she replied and sighed. "It's probably a crazy idea."

"What? You and Sean O'Sullivan? Well," Ellie teased gently, "it's not exactly obvious to the world, but it's not totally nuts. You like him, right?"

She nodded. "As I said, we're friends. Anything else feels like wishful thinking."

"The heart wants what the heart wants," Ellie said and smiled. "I hope it turns out how you want it to."

So did Leah. The thing was, although she'd talked a good line and flirted back, when it came to Sean, she really wasn't sure what she wanted. Involvement with anyone hadn't been on her radar. But their friendship had evolved so organically, *other* feelings had evolved with it. Feelings he clearly didn't share;

he'd made that abundantly clear. Whatever was happening between them, it was not serious. Because he didn't do serious. He didn't do love.

It was after eleven thirty when she considered calling it a night. The bride and groom had left half an hour earlier, and the caterers were collecting dishes and glasses. Matron of honor Tess and wedding planner extraordinaire Ellie were in complete control, so Leah collected her belongings and went looking for Sean. She found him by the bar, in conversation with two of her cousins. It made her smile. She knew her cousins liked and respected Kieran, since he'd helped both her dad and Mitch, but she knew there'd always been tension between the rest of the O'Sullivans and the Culhanes. Except both Grant and Joss were laughing and Sean was clearly keeping them entertained, or vice versa, and none of them appeared to be hanging out against their will.

When she approached, he took her bulging tote, and once they said goodbye, led her from the reception area and toward his car. There were a few vehicles remaining in the driveway, mostly trucks and SUVs, and Sean's red Ferrari stuck out like a beacon. Once her things were placed in the small trunk space, they headed off.

"It was a nice wedding," she remarked as they passed through the gates. "Don't you think?"

He nodded. "Sure."

"Annie looked so beautiful. I just love the way the tent was decorated. And those big electric fire things kept everyone warm and toasty. Plus the band was—"

"You're babbling," he said, not looking at her. "Do you know that your voice gets higher when you babble?"

Leah did know. She also knew she babbled when she was nervous. "Sorry."

She didn't say anything more and stared out the window, thinking how quiet the town was at night as they passed over the bridge and headed toward the river. When they reached their road, he turned into the shared driveway and fifty yards down eased the vehicle to a crawl.

"So, left or right?" he asked.

Leah swallowed hard. Left was her dad's place. Right was Sean's. He was giving her an out, an escape clause, and she suspected he wouldn't try to change her mind either way.

Because he's not invested...

The notion struck her hard, because she knew it was true. Sean liked her and had suddenly decided he wanted to have sex with her. But that was it. Despite the way her heart hammered and her insides jumped all over the place, it would never be anything more than sex between friends.

"Right," she said, figuring they were both single consenting adults and what harm would it do. Sure, she liked him, and he did make her pulse race and she did still have memories of the silly crush she'd had for him years earlier. But ultimately, her decision was about having the desire to live a little, to take a risk, to enjoy her life.

Sean didn't say a word and turned the car. When they arrived at his house, he used the remote to open the garage door and closed it once the car was tucked inside. He turned off the engine and got out.

"Do you need your bag?"

She had a change of clothes and toiletries in her tote, and considering what was happening, she figured she'd need both at some point. "Yes, thank you. I showered and changed into this dress at the ranch, so my real clothes are in my bag."

He pulled out her things and passed her the tote. "You look gorgeous, by the way."

Her mouth curved. "You look pretty damn nice yourself. Great suit."

Sean flicked on the lights as they walked through the house, and when they reached the large living room, Leah dropped her bag and faced him.

"Would you like a drink?" he asked.

"No."

"Food?"

She shook her head, nerves settling in her belly. "I've never been the casual sex type before," she admitted and gulped hard. "I had a college boyfriend and only two other serious relationships."

"While I have had nothing but casual sex, is what you're insinuating."

Leah didn't budge. "I'm not judging you."

He sighed. "The truth is, since my hearing has

deteriorated so much in the past twelve months, I haven't wanted to get involved with anyone. Too many questions. Too many explanations. Does that make sense?"

She nodded. "What about your landscape architect?"

"It lasted a few months," he replied and shrugged out of his jacket, dropping it on the back of the sofa. "And despite my best intentions, it felt casual. I think that's why we broke up. Cindy wanted something more...and I didn't have anything more to give."

"That's quite an admission."

"What? That I'm shallow and unable to commit? Maybe...but I want to be clear and honest with you, Leah. I don't want a relationship right now. But I don't want to mislead you."

"Believe me, Sean, your honesty is brutal and refreshing and not misleading in the slightest."

He moved around the couch. "I don't think I've ever known a woman quite like you. And you do look gorgeous in that dress."

"You said that already."

He grinned. "Because it's true. You're hard to ignore. And easy to like. It's quite a combination. A killer combo, actually," he said and stepped closer.

"What about the fact I'm not your go-to type?"

"You know, that's more about reputation than fact," he replied. "Right now, the only woman I'm interested in is you."

"Is that because I'm the only woman here?"

His gaze narrowed. "Do you think I'm that shallow?"

She shook her head a fraction. "No. But I think we're both alone, and probably lonely, and have somehow ended up in this moment together."

"Fate then?"

"Absolutely." Leah's insides jumped and she held out her hand. "Are you going to kiss me now?"

He grasped her hand and urged her toward him. "Oh, honey, if you'll let me, I'm going to do more than that."

Leah melted, her heart battering so hard against her rib cage she thought it might burst through her chest. He reached out and cupped her chin for a moment before removing the diamanté clip holding her hair in a loose roll.

"I've been wanting to do that all night," he admitted. "Your hair is too good to waste piled high like that," he said and threaded his fingers through the tresses. "It's very sexy hair."

"I didn't know hair could be sexy," she said with a shuddering breath, moving her face closer to his.

"Oh yeah," he said and held her nape gently. "It can. It is."

He angled her face up to his. Leah stared, thinking she'd never met a man with such brilliant blue eyes. The irises were arctic blue, circled by a darker shade, and with his thick lashes, the effect was riveting. She wondered how she'd ever find any man attractive again after Sean.

She felt his breath, cool against her mouth, and her lips parted instinctively. She'd been kissed before, but never with such intense anticipation, and when his mouth finally touched hers, she sighed so low in her throat it almost sounded like a moan. His mouth was magic, his tongue smooth as it wound around her own and he went deeper, not demanding, but asking. Leah let him in, feeling her heart rate increase and the blood in her veins hitched up several degrees.

So, yeah, the man knows how to kiss...

Big surprise...*not.*

Leah clutched his shoulders and sighed, pressing closer, feeling how the hard angles of his body fit so well against her, and any lingering doubts she had quickly disappeared. Of course, she knew she'd have regrets in the morning. She knew she was probably putting an end to their friendship...but damn, he felt so good and smelled so good and tasted so good... and she was just as human as the next woman. With the same needs. Maybe she'd put her libido on ice for the last couple of years, but it was well and truly thawed around Sean.

He lifted his head and grasped her chin. "Are you okay?"

Leah nodded. "Perfect."

Without another word, he grabbed her hand and led her upstairs. His bedroom was huge and had a deck that overlooked the river. It was a clear night, and she was surprised when he didn't close the curtains. Leah looked at the bed, a monstrous king-size thing covered in pale blue linens. She stood in the center of room, her feet suddenly stuck to the carpet, and she watched as he ditched his tie and loosened his collar. As much as she'd wanted to be with him, she felt an attack of nerves coming on.

"I'm not on the pill," she said flatly.

He moved in front of her, pulling his shirt from the waistband of his trousers. "I've never had unprotected sex in my life, Leah," he said and walked to the bed, opening up the bedside drawer and extracting an unopened box of condoms. "I'm not about to start now."

She was relieved. Of course unprotected sex was out of the question. She'd never been careless with birth control. And a baby would be a disaster. Of course she wanted children one day. Once she was in a committed relationship with a man she loved and who loved her in return. But she was under no illusions about Sean. This was sex. Nothing more.

She watched, fascinated as he flipped off his shoes and began unbuttoning his shirt. Leah dropped the wrap around her shoulders. "Unzip me," she said and turned.

He walked behind her and slowly inched the zipper down her spine, kissing one shoulder and then the other. The dress fell to her feet and she shivered, even though there was enough heat in the room to start a forest fire.

"Turn around," he said, his breath warm against her neck.

Leah had always kept herself in shape and didn't have too many body image issues, but when she turned to face him, she was instantly conscious of the padded satin bra that pushed her breasts upward and added considerable inches to her bustline.

"My one attempt at vanity," she admitted and met his gaze.

"No need," he said and ran a hand along her shoulder.

"I don't have long legs or blond hair," she said and dropped her head to one side. "I'm not…beautiful."

He reached out and cupped her cheek, tracing his thumb along her bottom lip. "That's the funny thing about beauty, Leah. It really is in the eye of the beholder," he said and gathered her close. "And since, right this minute, I'm the one looking at you, you really are taking my breath away."

If it was a line, she didn't care. Leah had never felt more desirable in her life. She stepped on her toes and kissed him, hotly, deeply, thrusting her tongue into his mouth like she'd wanted to do for weeks, and he kissed her back with so much skill she was almost knocked off her feet.

She couldn't remember how they got to the bed, or how their clothes were stripped off. She only recalled his touch, and the reverence in every stroke of his fingertips and every plunge of his tongue in her mouth. And the way he caressed her skin, the way his lips felt against her breasts and how erotic it was to feel his tongue laving her nipples. Leah had had good sex before. But not like this. Sean knew exactly where to touch her—he knew places that drove her crazy with desire. He kissed her in places she'd forgotten could be kissed. He found erogenous zones she never knew she possessed. He knew how to make her moan and writhe and finally beg for release. And he clearly liked the way she explored him with her mouth and hands. He was encouraging, not demanding, allowing her to take the lead in between hot, deep kisses that took her to a fever pitch and made her crave to touch him everywhere. His skin was so smooth, his muscled body lean and tanned. She kissed his chest, his shoulders, his smooth washboard belly, touching him without hesitation.

He caressed her gently and expertly, bringing her to the brink countless times.

"Please?" she begged, panting in between shuddering breaths.

He kissed the sensitive spot below her earlobe, whispering something shockingly intimate, something that should have made her toes curl but instead amplified the desire churning through her blood. He grabbed a condom from the box and quickly sheathed himself, moving over her.

"Is this okay?" he asked softly, settling between her legs.

Leah nodded, looking directly into his eyes. "Wonderful."

And it was wonderful. Every movement was pure pleasure, every kiss an erotic journey of the senses. White-hot heat enveloped her and she clung to him as they rode the wave together, holding his shoulders, urging him toward the release they both clearly craved. When it came, she moaned his name, meeting his gaze face-to-face, which in some ways felt much more intimate than the joining of their bodies.

When it was over, he kissed her mouth softly and rolled away, discreetly disappearing in the adjoining bathroom for a moment. She looked at the clock on the bedside table—2:43 a.m. They'd made love for over two hours.

Had sex.

She corrected herself instantly, refusing to get swept up in some romantic fantasy about what was happening between them. He'd made his thoughts very clear. When he returned to the room, Leah was lying on her side, the sheet pulled up a little, her head supported by one hand. She admired him openly in the lamplight, taking her time to appreciate the muscle stretched over bone, his broad shoulders and chest and the patch of hair between his pectorals.

"You'll make me blush," he said as he approached the bed, "if you keep looking at me like that."

Leah raised her brows appreciatively and met his gaze. "You really are ridiculously attractive."

He laughed. "You're not so bad yourself."

She didn't quite believe him, but it was a happy

fairy tale to tell herself one day. "Thank you. That was…nice."

His brow rose questioningly. "Nice?"

She grinned, and her limbs began to pulse when he joined her in the bed and scooted close, wrapping one strong arm around her, his semi-aroused state very obvious. "Well, I don't want to inflate your ego too much."

"Why not?" he teased. "If we can't brag to one another, then who can we brag to? I don't kiss and tell."

"Speaking of kissing," she said and raised her lips to his, "how about you do that crazy hot thing you do with your tongue again."

He smiled sexily. "Which thing?"

Leah placed her mouth against his and traced her tongue along the edge of his lower lip. "*That* thing."

He grabbed her hands and laughed, taking her mouth in a splendidly erotic kiss that was quickly a precursor to another lovemaking session. Quicker, this time, and hotter, if that were possible. When it was over they fell asleep in an exhausted tangle of arms and legs, and she didn't stir again until nearly six o'clock. It was still dark outside, and Leah smiled when she realized she was tucked, spoon fashion, in the curve of Sean's body as he slept.

She wasn't sure what to do with the jumble of emotions wreaking havoc with her good sense. She didn't want to believe she was foolish enough to be falling in love with him. Love was not in the cards for either of them.

It's transitional sex, that's all.

For Leah because she was trying to purge all thoughts of Xavier from her heart and head, and for Sean because he was beginning a new life in Cedar River and she was a convenient diversion from him having to tell his family why he'd come back.

It's just sex, remember that.

She moved and he rolled, flipping onto his stomach, his features barely visible in the darkened room, but somehow in the course of the last few hours, she had memorized them. *Like a love-sick fool.* She pushed the thought off and looked at him. In sleep he seemed so peaceful, without a frown etching his forehead, without tension setting his mouth in a grim line. Leah touched his hair, twirling the dark strands between her fingertips, finally settling the backs of her fingers against his jaw. She felt the stubble of his beard and remembered how shaggy it had been when they'd first met. Weeks ago, but it seemed longer, as though they'd been friends for considerable time.

And now they were lovers.

She sighed, thinking hard, thinking that she'd probably made a stupid mistake, and then remembered how great making love with him had been and couldn't feel one tiny tinge of regret.

Leah slid out of bed and looked around for her things, remembering that she'd left her bag downstairs. She grabbed the first thing she could find—his shirt—and slipped it on, rolling up the sleeves before she quickly headed from the bedroom.

The kitchen light was on, and realizing she was parched, she found a glass and drank some water. The sun had started to rise, and she looked through the wide window, noticing a couple of boats moored at jetties on the river. The morning view from her dad's place wasn't anywhere near as peaceful, and she sighed, relaxing a little.

"Are you coming back to bed?"

Sean's voice startled her, and she swiveled on her heels. He wore a robe, loosely tied around his waist, his hair disheveled, his eyes hooded and sleepy. "I should probably go home."

His gaze traveled over her slowly. "In that outfit?"

She looked down at his shirt. "It was the first thing I found."

"What?" he asked, his tone sharper.

"I said it was the first thing—"

"It would help if you could face me when you speak," he reminded her. "Unless we're...you know... close."

Guilt pushed down on her shoulders. "I know, I should have remembered. I didn't mean to look away," she said, enunciating clearer.

"And don't do that, either," he snapped and then shook his head. "Sorry, I didn't... I'm sorry, Leah."

Her heart ached. "I can't promise to always get it right, but I'd never intentionally offend you or treat you differently."

"I know," he said and sighed heavily. "But I'm still coming to terms with everything I'm going to lose and everything I have to learn. And I just… I need to do this at my own pace, and some of this isn't in my control."

Of course she knew that. "Maybe if you talked to someone, it might help."

"I *am* talking to someone," he reminded her.

She swallowed hard. "I meant, someone like… your brother Kieran. He's a wonderful doctor and I'm sure he would understand—"

"I'll pick you up at two o'clock…if you still plan on coming with me today," he said quickly, cutting her off.

"Of course," she said.

She was walking out of the house about ten minutes later, dressed in the jeans, a sweater, a fleecy jacket and boots she had in her tote. Sean offered to accompany her on the short walk back to her dad's, but she declined, needing the crisp morning air to clear her head and thoughts. He didn't try to kiss her goodbye. In fact, he didn't touch her again before she left. Which was fine. They'd had their night together. The daytime made everything clearer.

Betty and Wilma greeted her by the front door when she let herself into the house. She was tired, and needed a shower and a nap, but as Leah headed for her room, her father snagged her attention by calling to her from his favorite chair in the living room. She hovered in the doorway.

"Did you stay at the ranch last night?" he asked.

Leah tried not to look like a guilty seventeen-year-old sneaking in after curfew. "Not exactly."

Her dad looked at her over the top of his reading glasses. "Should I stop asking questions?"

She nodded. "I think so."

"All right," he replied. "Just be careful. I fed the dogs in case you were wondering."

"Thanks, Dad."

She headed for her room, dumped her bag and flopped onto the bed.

And then, despite telling herself to keep it together, she cried.

Because she knew, despite all her best intentions, that she'd fallen head over heels for a man who said he didn't believe in love.

Chapter Eight

"I appreciate you doing this," Sean said as they headed into town and toward the hotel that afternoon. He saw Leah nod her agreement. She looked lovely in a long-sleeved blue dress. Her hair was down, and its magical colors shimmered every time she moved.

He spotted his mother, Liam and Kayla once they were in the hotel foyer, and his brother waved to him. They greeted Leah as though seeing them together was the most normal thing in the world, and he wasn't sure if he was irked or pleased.

"By the way," Liam said as they walked toward one of the convention rooms. "I'm stepping back from this one. It's just you and Jonah doing speeches for Dad today," he said and motioned to Jonah, who was standing just inside the doorway with Kieran.

Sean stopped in his tracks and glared at his older brother. "What?"

Liam grinned. "That way you two can bond."

Sean felt Leah's hand touch his arm and she leaned in toward him. "It'll be okay," she said softly, but was close enough that he heard every word.

Sean looked at Jonah and noticed the other man was frowning. In that moment he realized how much alike he and Jonah were. Hell, they even looked alike. There was no mistaking the fact they were brothers. And they both had a tendency for bad-tempered silences.

"When is Dad getting here?" he asked, looking around at the perfectly decorated room. The tables were set. There were balloons and a huge painted sign wishing J.D. the happiest of birthdays.

"My mom said she'd get him by three," Jonah replied and Sean glanced at his own mother.

As strong and stoic as Gwen appeared, he knew she put considerable effort into keeping up the appearance that she was doing *just fine*. But Sean wasn't entirely convinced.

"You okay, Mom?" he asked once Jonah and the rest of his family moved away.

She nodded, her back straight, her eyes clear. "I'm good, honey. Don't worry about me."

"I do worry," he said quietly and felt Leah's fingers tighten reassuringly around his arm. "But if you say you're fine, then I'll believe you."

Gwen patted his shoulder. "Thanks for being so sweet," she said and then looked at Leah. "Make him have a good time today, will you?"

Leah smiled and he noticed her cheeks were pink. "I'll do my best."

Strangely, having Leah beside him was comforting, her silent support somehow a tangible force. He couldn't explain it and didn't want to dissect it. He only knew he was glad she was there.

Of course everything between them felt different. For one, all he could think about was making love with her again. It had been quite a night, filled with passion and pleasure and even laughter. Although her hasty departure had bothered him, he wasn't about to labor over it. He knew men and women thought about sex differently. And Leah was very much a deep-feeling woman. Perhaps she simply needed some time to put what had happened between them into perspective, as he had. It was plain old-fashioned hot sex between two people who liked one another.

And he wanted more of her.

J.D. arrived at three o'clock and was clearly stunned by the celebration. The reception was catered to perfection by Abby Culhane, the head chef. Sean remembered Abby from high school and knew she was married to Leah's cousin Jake. Sean did his best to mingle, managing to avoid getting too caught up in any long conversations he couldn't navigate in the crowd. The seating was fluid, and people were moving around the room. Sean spotted Leah speaking with his mother and quickly joined them.

"Everything okay?" he asked.

Leah nodded. "I was just telling your mother about how I'm thinking of having a showing."

"Not thinking," he corrected. "Doing."

She shrugged. "Until my insecurity kicks in."

His mother said something he couldn't quite decipher, and he found himself leaning closer toward Leah, who seemed to take the cue and responded.

"Yes, Gwen," she replied. "I agree that Sean will be a great help."

And then, in his usual blustering style, J.D. approached and joined their circle. His father was big, broad and still carried himself with the energy of a much younger man. He was larger than life, sometimes loud and obnoxious, often disliked but never taken for a fool. He had more money than he could ever spend and more gall than was considered socially acceptable. Like him or loathe him, J. D. O'Sullivan was a man who once met, was never forgotten.

Sean introduced him to Leah, quickly realized that she had met him before and waited for his father's inevitable and inappropriate comment. And wasn't disappointed.

"About time you ditched the bimbos and spent time with someone who has a brain."

He saw Leah's face leach of color. "Be cool, Dad."

"I'm just saying," J.D. said and slapped him affectionately on the shoulder. "Brains trump beauty every time."

"Come with me, Leah," his mother said. She cleverly cut between them, gathered Leah by the elbow and led her away. "Excuse us, we have an art showing to plan."

Once they were out of range, Sean turned to face his father. "Really? Could you be a bigger jerk?"

He made a face. "I was paying you a compliment."

"By insulting my date?"

"I didn't mean to insult her," J.D. said and frowned. "In fact, I think it's a huge improvement. Smart *and* pretty. Let's face it, in the past, smart never figured high on your list of priorities when it came to women."

Sean's blood simmered. "Since I've been living in another state for the last decade, I'm not sure how you'd know that."

"I hear things," J.D. replied. "I'm just saying, she's an improvement."

"She has a name," Sean shot back. "It's Leah. And we're friends, that's all."

"That's because you're scared of commitment," his father said bluntly.

Or at least that's what Sean thought he said. He wasn't sure. And since Leah wasn't around to back it up, he shrugged angrily. "I don't think it lasts. Let's be honest, Dad, you're a walking and talking example of how to fail at commitment—since you cheated on your wife and had a secret family tucked away for thirty years."

J.D.'s face turned red. "Do you think this is the place to have this conversation?"

"No," Sean replied. "Because it's not a conversation I want to have at all. Anyway, I have to get going. I'll see you around."

J.D. grabbed his forearm. "I don't want us to be at odds over this, son. Everyone else has been able to forgive me and move on, even your mother and Jonah…why can't you?"

Sean shrugged off his father's viselike grip as discreetly as he could. "So it's forgiveness you want?"

"I want peace," J.D. replied. "I thought we finally had that as a family. But you…you seem incapable of it, and I don't understand why. Did all those years away from us destroy your ability to remember that we *are* a family…faults and all? Frankly, hiding away in that big house, barely talking to any of us, that's no way to be a part of things. I think it's what a spoiled brat would do."

Sean was furious, but he wouldn't lose his temper while surrounded by so many people. For one, with so many conversations going on around him, it all seemed like white noise and was suddenly stifling. He looked around for Leah, found her by the buffet table with his mother and excused himself with a dismissive wave and took off.

Gwen saw him first and patted his arm once he

joined them. "Darling, you have to learn to get along with your dad."

"I know, Mom," he said and sighed. "Just not today." He looked at Leah. "Sorry about that."

She grinned. "I think you were more offended than me." She shrugged. "Don't worry about it."

He figured he'd overreacted. But damn, he didn't want anyone insulting her. Not when he…when he… His thoughts froze. Okay, so he was being stupidly overprotective, and he shouldn't allow anyone to get under his skin. And he figured J.D. really didn't mean any harm.

"So, have you and Mom worked out a date for your showing?"

"After Christmas," she replied quickly.

"Before Christmas," Gwen corrected. "And after Thanksgiving. I'll make sure the gallery is free."

"I'm not convinced," Leah said and sighed.

His mother said something he didn't catch and he looked at Leah, amazed how easily she picked up on his distress at not hearing his mother's words.

"That would be great," Leah said and smiled. "I'd love some of your cranberry jelly."

Gwen nodded approvingly, but thinking about the holidays made his jaw ache. He knew Kieran was hosting Thanksgiving, and everyone would be there. After that, it would be Christmas and New Year's. He'd make an effort, buy gifts, spend time with the kids and fake it until people believed he was happy to be there. For the thousandth time, Sean wished

Liz was still alive. His sister understood him. And being back in Cedar River only amplified how much he missed her.

The speeches were done once the huge birthday cake was cut, and Sean did his best to keep his words short and to the point, mentioning his father's achievements and how much he'd done for the town, steering clear of anything personal. Jonah's speech was a little more family friendly, and he was relieved that the reception was over about an hour later, pleased to finally be able to get away.

"Do you want me to drive to your dad's?" he asked when they were almost home.

She shrugged. "If that's what you want."

"I'm asking what you want. I'm happy to hang with you some more," he added and smiled a little. "If that's what *you* want."

She nodded and he headed down his driveway. Once they were in the house, Sean turned on the heater in the electric fireplace and offered to make coffee.

"The party was a success," she said and stood on the other side of the long countertop. "And you were mostly well behaved."

Sean grabbed a couple of mugs. "That doesn't sound like a compliment, exactly."

She looked amused. "I did say *mostly*. But you have a great family—maybe you should try harder to get along."

Sean wanted to be annoyed by her words, but

knew she had a point. "I think they work better without me around."

"Nonsense," she said. "Your mom already told me you were her favorite."

He laughed and the sensation eased some of the tension rumbling in his chest. "Well, you can't blame her for that. Liam's such a stick-in-the-mud and Kieran is way too nice. I've been told I'm rather charming."

"You can be," she said and chuckled, then regarded him more seriously. "You know, my grandmother Mitti wears a hearing aid. It's this tiny little thing that's hardly noticeable. Maybe you could talk to her about it."

"I'd rather keep my personal life private and—"

"I didn't mean to suggest that I've said anything to anyone," she said, cutting him off. "You told me about your condition in confidence and I haven't betrayed that, even though I don't like keeping secrets from my dad. All I'm suggesting is you consider having a conversation with someone who has been through something similar."

Logically, he knew she was right. Talking about it *would* most likely help. But…something held him back. Pride perhaps? Or a rising sense of emasculation. Whatever it was, he knew he didn't want to talk with strangers. "Are you doing anything Tuesday?" he asked abruptly. "I have an appointment with a specialist in Rapid City."

"And you could use the company of a friend?"

He nodded. "Yes, I could."

She took a moment, almost as though she was deciding something important. "Sure."

"Thank you."

And that, he thought, was that.

Leah had no illusions about her relationship with Sean. She wasn't even sure she should be thinking in terms of *relationship*. So, yes, she ended up in bed with him late on Sunday afternoon, and yes, she was going with him to Rapid City on Tuesday. But that was it. The incredible sex was addling her brain.

She spent most of Monday in the barn, working on a couple of unfinished pieces, and after lunch talked to her dad about his physical therapy. Sean texted her around two and once she knew Ivan was settled with his tea in front of the television, Leah headed to Sean's. They made love again, as she knew they would, and he walked her home late in the afternoon, a couple of steps behind her. They were both surprised to see Gwen's car parked in the driveway.

"Are you going to behave yourself?" she asked once she turned to face him.

He stopped moving. "What?"

"You mom is here, spending time with my dad… you know how overprotective you get."

"I'm fine," he said casually. "I like your dad."

"Dating your mother?"

His jaw tightened. "Is that what they're doing?"

She shrugged and opened the front door. "I'm not

sure. But I know my dad seems happier these days, so that makes me happy."

His mouth curled and he grabbed her hand. "Oh, that's what's making you happy?"

Leah's belly did a silly flip. *Don't be a fool, he's flirting, that's all.* "Well, I have to admit the last few days have been unexpectedly...interesting."

He hauled her closer, bringing their bodies into contact. "Are we still friends?"

"Of course."

"I'd hate that to change, you know," he said and cupped her nape, gently anchoring her head. "I've never had a friend quite like you."

"Me, either," she admitted.

He smiled and kissed her hotly, lingering around the edges of her lips as his free hand molded her hip. Leah sighed against his mouth, fighting the inevitable hunger that wound through her blood, and quickly lost the battle. She wasn't sure how long they stood like that—minutes, probably seconds, but it was her father's familiar throat-clearing sound that pulled her back. Sean took a few more seconds to register that they had an audience and managed to quickly find a more suitable place for his hands other than her behind.

"Ah—Gwen is in the kitchen," Ivan said, looking a little more disapproving than she would have imagined and then put it down to being a typical parent.

Leah bit down on her reddened bottom lip. "Thanks, Dad."

Gwen regarded them even more curiously and didn't hold back her opinion. "I hope you're not going to make a mess of this," she said, looking directly at her son.

To his credit, Sean didn't flinch. Leah knew how much love and respect he had for his mother and suspected he'd never show his annoyance. "I'll do my best not to."

Gwen nodded. "Can you come to my place tomorrow morning? I have a couple of pieces of furniture I want to give to Goodwill, and I need some help moving them."

"Sorry, Mom, I'm busy tomorrow," he replied as they sat down at the table. "But I can drop by Wednesday."

"Busy?"

Leah saw his expression sharpen and quickly jumped in. "Ah, we're heading into Rapid City tomorrow," she said and then noticed that he looked horrified that she was going to out him. "I left a few boxes of things with my neighbor when I moved from my apartment last month, and Sean promised to help me get them."

Gwen accepted her explanation and kept busy making coffee. She and Ivan were quite the pair as they moved around the kitchen, and it made Leah smile. She liked seeing her dad happy, and Gwen was a lovely woman.

"Sean, cream and sugar?"

Ivan's voice was clear and precise, but Sean didn't

respond and Leah saw that he was looking down, clearly immersed in his own thoughts. She tapped his foot with her own under the table and he quickly looked up.

"What?"

"Sean," Gwen said sharply. "What on earth is going on with you these days? It's like you zone out even when people are trying to talk to you."

He got to his feet in a microsecond. "Sorry, Mom, I just have things on my mind. I'll rain check the coffee."

Leah met his gaze and clearly understood the look in his eyes.

I'll rain check, us, too...

He excused himself, leaving the room abruptly— and his mother clearly confused.

Once the front door opened and closed, Leah looked toward Gwen, and the older woman was regarding her with concern. "Leah, if you know what's wrong with my son, please tell me."

Leah took a breath and stood. "I'm sorry...but I can't do that."

Gwen's concerned looked amplified. "He's struggling with something, and I feel so shut out. But he trusts you, and you obviously have become close. Please tell me I'm worrying without cause."

"I can't do that, either."

The older woman looked grave. "Is he sick?"

Leah waved a hand. "Please don't ask me. I can't talk about it. But I will speak to him and encourage him to talk to you."

Of course she knew that Sean would think that was an intrusion on his privacy, and she certainly didn't want to be between him and his family, particularly his mother. Gwen was a friend.

But Sean was so much more.

Leah headed for her studio and continued sorting through her completed pieces. There were seven large sculptures in total. She knew some of them were her best work, several done in copper and brass. With the selection of pottery pieces and some of her more eclectic metalwork, Leah knew she had enough inventory to have a show. There were even a couple of abstract canvasses she'd done a couple of years earlier.

She examined the pieces and tried to summon her courage…but truthfully, she was terrified of having another failed show. The last time only a handful of people had turned up, and the caterers were left wrapping uneaten food and beverages. It had been the most humiliating moment of her life, and one she didn't want to repeat. But if she didn't have another show, then she'd never know if she had the talent to make it. Her dad and David believed in her. So did Gwen. And Sean believed in her, too.

Leah grabbed her cell and sent him a message.

Do you want some company?

She waited a few minutes for his reply.

Sure.

It wasn't exactly encouraging, but she pushed her cell into her pocket, grabbed her coat and walked to his house. He was waiting on the porch when she arrived, grabbing her hand once she climbed the stairs.

"Are you okay?" she asked.

"Yeah. I guess."

"You upset your mom," she said bluntly.

He shrugged. "I wasn't in the mood to explain myself, particularly in front of other people."

Other people...

He said the words as though she was as unimportant as a mere acquaintance. But then he pulled her close, and her irritation disappeared.

I'm so predictable.

"Are you staying tonight?"

"For a while. I thought we could talk about the showing," she said and pulled back. "If you have time."

"I have time," he said, looking at her with blistering intensity. "Time is something I have in abundance these days."

Ten minutes later, once they were inside and sitting in the living room on opposite ends of the sofa, Leah was convinced that a show was the worst idea of the century.

"I don't know who to invite," she said and sighed.

"Let's start with the basics," he remarked. "Who is your target audience?"

She shrugged. "I don't know...people who like metal artwork."

"What kind of people?" he asked. "You have a great deal of talent, and your pieces are not only thoughtfully designed and clearly a part of you. Let's use that to our advantage. Think about *who* you want to see your work."

He grabbed his laptop, and they spent the following hour talking about a potential guest list and then going over the pieces she considered to be her best and which ones would be showcased as a priority in the exhibition. He made a few suggestions about her selection and then listened to her protests when he recommended she leave her pottery work for another time.

"I understand what you're saying," he said quietly, pushing the laptop aside. "What I'm suggesting is that you don't want to send a mixed message. Imagine if your favorite country singer suddenly recorded a jazz song. Confusing, right? And when you're developing your craft, when you're trying to get an audience, you want to give that audience what they expect."

"But my pottery pieces are part of my craft," she insisted. "An important part."

"And yet not the centerpiece," he remarked. "Not like your metalwork, particularly since you now have a significant sample of that in the hotel foyer. Your metalwork and your paintings—they should be what you showcase this time. Sometimes, more is simply *more*."

Leah was about to protest again, but bit the words back. "I'm still not sure this is a good idea," she said.

His gaze narrowed. "Because you're scared of failure?"

She nodded. "Of course I'm scared. I'm terrified. What if no one turns up? What if I'm left humiliated and embarrassed and left with nowhere to hide?"

Sean grabbed her hand. "Leah, people will come," he insisted. "And you do incredible work so you won't be humiliated or embarrassed. And," he added, gently squeezing her hand, "if you need somewhere to hide, you can hide behind me."

It was a nice idea, but Leah wasn't about to read too much into his words. He was being kind, and for some reason of his own, he wanted to help her. "I know you're trying to help, but if the same thing happens as last time, I think it will make me quit pursuing art forever."

He didn't release her. "Trust me, okay?"

Her eyes widened. She knew why she was resistant to go with his judgment...*trust*. For a long time she'd talked herself out of trusting anyone. It was safer to hold on to her mistrust and wrap it around herself like a cloak than to let someone in. And her feelings were now made even more complicated because of their current relationship.

"You know I want to but—"

"You said you only trust two men," he said, finishing the sentence for her. "Your dad and your brother. But I'm not saying this stuff to deceive you, Leah. I'm not saying this because I have some secret agenda. I'm not about to steal from you or mislead you. I want to help you succeed. Frankly, if you can't trust me, then we *should* forget this idea."

She sucked in a breath. "I do trust you," she admitted. "I mean, I wouldn't have…you know…" Her words trailed off and she colored hotly.

"I'm not sure having sex with someone and trusting them go hand in hand."

"For me, it does," she said and pulled away, getting to her feet. "Perhaps I'm not as accustomed to casual sex as you are? Because that's what we're doing, right?"

He looked at her, his gaze penetrating and then suddenly impatient. "Are we about to have an argument?"

"I think so."

Sean sighed heavily and stood. "Okay, let me have it. You obviously have something on your mind, so I'd rather we lay it out."

"I don't," she retorted, crossing her arms. "It's just that sometimes you just…" She paused deliberately. "Well, you just think like a guy."

He didn't flinch. Didn't react. He looked mildly amused, if anything. After a moment he moved around the sofa. "Are you staying for dinner?"

"No," she replied, arms still crossed, chin high,

because she knew *dinner* was code for *sex*. "I'll see you tomorrow, if you still want me to come with you."

His expression hardened a little, and then he shrugged. "Sure. I'll pick you up at ten."

Leah left quickly, her heart aching so much she had to hold a hand to her chest to ease the pain. He really was unbearable sometimes. Sure, he was helping her with the showing, but she suspected he simply wanted something to fill his time, to take his mind off his own troubles and maybe she was his pet project.

Well, fine. If he wanted to help her, she'd jump on board. She'd wanted to have a successful career, and Sean knew all about having one of those. She'd be a fool to refuse his help and not listen to his expertise. That decision helped her make another one—she wasn't going to sleep with him again. She knew her odds of falling in love with him amplified now that they had made love. Not that it *was* making love. He kept calling it sex and she needed to do the same.

She absolutely wasn't going to get her heart broken. Not again.

Chapter Nine

When his car pulled into her driveway Tuesday morning, Leah had had plenty of time to galvanize her resolve and convince herself she was doing the smart thing by ending things with Sean. Not their friendship, because that wasn't likely to leave her emotionally bruised. But being lovers was out of the question. There was no romantic happily-ever-after on the horizon, and she'd realized that was exactly what she wanted. She didn't want a casual sexual relationship with anyone...least of all a man who she had developed feelings for. It was better this way. Just friends. Friends she could handle. Friends wouldn't break her heart.

"Hi," she said as she got into his car, looking directly at him. "It's a beautiful morning."

That was true. The sky was clear, crystalline blue and the mountains had never looked greener. Leah loved South Dakota in the fall and would never want to call anywhere else home. Not like Sean, of course, who she suspected still pined for the warmth of California and its golden beaches.

"Yes, pretty perfect."

"I thought we might check out a couple of the art galleries in Rapid City while we're there, if that's okay?"

He nodded and turned out of the driveway. "No problem."

She made some idle small talk at the start of the forty-minute drive to Rapid City, but by the end of the trip she was content to be quiet and look out the window. Leah had worked in the town for a couple of years and had mostly enjoyed her time there, however she was glad to be back home in Cedar River for the foreseeable future.

Sean easily navigated his way through the streets and pulled into a parking space outside a private specialist medical practice. Once inside they took the elevator to the third floor and to the audiologist. A few people were seated in the waiting area, and Leah stood back while Sean spoke to the receptionist. Once they were seated she looked around, noticing a young mother sitting a few seats away. She had two sons, one of whom wore a pair of hearing aids. Leah smiled at the woman, who returned the gesture. An elderly couple sat opposite them, and Leah smiled in their direction too. Sean, she noticed, wasn't smiling. He looked positively pensive, his jaw set tightly, his mouth a grim line. She fought the urge to hold his hand. Did friends hold hands? For whatever reason, he'd invited her, so that gave her some privilege. She patted his arm reassuringly and then noticed him shift uncomfortably in his chair. He hated sympathy. And pity. And reassurance of any kind, because he believed that made him weak. Stupid man.

He was called up a few minutes later, and Leah remained where she was as he was ushered down the hall and into another room. Leah busied herself chatting to the young mother for a while, until she and her children were called up for their appointment. After that she flipped through magazines and then looked at her social media on her cell when the receptionist came toward her.

"Your husband has finished his testing and is now in room 4," the woman said and smiled. "You can join him there."

"Oh, he's not my…" Her words trailed off and she waved a hand. Maybe they wouldn't allow her in if they thought she wasn't his wife? That was a chance she wasn't about to take. "Thank you."

Leah got to her feet and walked down the corridor, quickly finding room 4. She opened the door and immediately spotted Sean sitting on a chair in front of a desk, his hand clenched in his lap, his back straight and tight.

She stood beside the vacant chair near him. "The receptionist said I could come in here," she explained. "Is that okay with you?"

He nodded. "Sure."

"How was the testing?" she asked.

"I guess I'll find out soon enough," he replied. "The test itself was the same as the last one I had—a soundproof room, a headset and negotiating my way through a series of beeps, and then they read words to you while covering their mouth."

The door opened and a tall, striking man appeared. "Good morning, I'm Dr. Gao."

For the next few minutes, the doctor explained the results of Sean's test and compared it to the same test he'd had in Los Angeles. It wasn't great news. There was significant deterioration, and the long-term prognosis was that it would continue to get worse over time.

"I can prescribe and fit hearing aids now," the doctor suggested. "It's your decision."

"No," Sean said. "Not yet."

Dr. Gao's face creased with a frown and he glanced toward Leah, his expression softening. "Perhaps you would like to discuss it together and alone."

"Oh," Leah said quickly. "We're not a couple," she said and then foolishly felt her face grow hotter. "I mean…we're…"

Sean grasped her hand and linked their fingers.

"We don't need to explain anything," he said and got to his feet, dragging Leah with him. "Thank you. I'll be in touch when I feel it's necessary."

"You know, the devices are small and discreet," Dr. Gao said and nodded. "And barely noticeable. But they will make a significant difference to your hearing."

"I'm sure they will," Sean replied, still holding her hand in a firm grip. "I'll let you know."

"And I'll have reception make a follow-up appointment in a couple of weeks," the other man said.

Once they were out of the office and striding down the corridor, he finally released her hand. By the time they got to his car, Leah knew he was pissed.

"Something wrong?" she asked.

He glared at her. "You know, I didn't ask you along today so you could flirt with the doctor."

Leah laughed. He actually sounded jealous. "I didn't lie. We're not a couple."

"I know that," he said shortly and opened the door for her. "You made that abundantly clear when you took off Sunday afternoon."

Leah stared at him and longed to mutter something coarse under her breath, but didn't want to appear mean and say things she knew he wouldn't be able to hear. "You set the rules, Sean, remember? You said you weren't looking for anything serious and that we were just going to sleep together and be friends with benefits."

"You said you didn't want anything serious, ei-ther," he reminded her as he started the engine.

"I don't," she fibbed, stunned that they were hav-ing such a conversation. "And I wasn't flirting with the doctor. He was just trying to help. And clearly thinks you need to consider getting the hearing aids."

He banged a hand on the steering wheel. "I *said* I'm not ready for that yet."

She didn't flinch. Because he sounded so utterly vulnerable beneath his anger, Leah's irritation sub-sided immediately. "But Sean," she said and touched his arm. "At some point, knowing your family, they'll probably have an intervention and you'll be forced to tell them what's going on. Wouldn't you rather tell them on your own terms?"

"Then I'll just stay out of their way until I'm ready," he said.

"You're being a little stubborn," she stated and huffed out an impatient breath.

"What?" he asked, frowning.

Leah repeated her words, then added, "And stub-borness is a flaw, by the way. The art gallery is that way," she said and hitched a thumb in the other di-rection. "You promised."

"I know," he said and sighed. "I really don't like fighting with you, Leah. Although," he added and smiled, "it could be a good reason to have make up sex."

"Oh no," she said the words with a fiery glare. "We not having sex anymore."

"We're not?"

"No," she replied. "It will just be friendship and business."

"Business?"

"Yes," she said and smiled tightly. "The business of my art showing. Unless you've changed your mind?"

"I haven't changed my mind," he said and drove into the parking area in front of the art gallery. "You're the one who seems to do that."

Leah rallied her resolve and decided the best decision she'd ever made was the one to get their relationship back to platonic. Except, of course, later that afternoon, once they were back in Cedar River and at his house, she tumbled straight into bed with him again for several hours of passionate, uninhibited, mind-blowing sex. Afterward she was exhausted and completely out her mind with wanting him. And needing him. And loving him.

So much for platonic.

When Sean arrived at his mother's place on Wednesday, both his brothers were sitting in the kitchen. Of course he knew his mother had probably arranged the whole scene. He uttered an irritated greeting and was forced to listen to several minutes of pointless chitchat before Liam, who always got to the point with things, asked him a direct question.

"Are you sick?"

Sean's back straightened. "Do I look it?"

Kieran interjected in his best physician's tone. "No, but there could be—"

"I'm not sick," Sean replied irritably. "I don't have cancer, or lupus or heart disease or anything like that," he said, looking at his mother. "So, relax, I'm fine."

Kieran's gaze narrowed. "What about addiction?"

Sean stilled instantly, looking at the concerned faces of the three other people in the room. Jesus, they actually thought he might be on the wagon from dependency of some narcotic. It was too ridiculous for words. He rarely drank, loathed cigarettes, hadn't smoked weed since his early twenties and had never touched any other drug, even though it was readily available. His friends and colleagues had called him uptight and too straight and boring…but that scene had never interested him. He'd left Cedar River to get a life, not wreck his life.

He laughed loudly. "I'm not detoxing, either. I know you think everyone who lives in LA is a drug addict, but that's not the case, I assure you."

"Of course we don't think that," Kieran said and sighed. "But your behavior since you've been back could indicate—"

"What exactly do you want me to say?" he interrupted and got to his feet. "Look, I'm not like the rest of you, okay. I don't have that *family first* gene ingrained in my DNA. I liked my life in LA. I liked the work I did and the money I made and the house I lived in by the beach and the friends I had. But now

I'm here, and I don't want the third degree about *why* every time I see you guys."

"Getting angry isn't helping," Kieran said—or at least that's what Sean thought he'd said.

"I'm not angry," he replied, irritated by his brother's calm and even tone. "But you all need to back off."

"We can't," Liam said, shaking his head. "You're family and like you said, for us, family comes first. I was thinking that maybe you'd like to come and work at the hotel. Connie begins her maternity leave at the end of this week and the assistant manager's job is available."

Sean rolled his eyes. "I don't know anything about running a hotel."

"You can learn," his brother said. "And I really want to step back a bit more now that Kayla and I have two kids. What do you say?"

Heat snaked up his spine. "No, thanks. I don't need a job."

"You need something," Kieran said. "Working might be a good diversion."

"From what?"

"From whatever it is that's haunting you."

It was his mother's voice he heard—clear and obviously concerned. Sean let out a long breath and walked to his mother, hugging her briefly. "I'm fine, Mom. Looks like you have enough muscle here to help you move that furniture. I'll see you later."

He left and headed into town, tamping down his

irritation and keeping his foot off the gas to ensure he didn't get a speeding ticket. He dropped by the hardware store and ordered some more paint and then stopped at the supermarket to pick up a few things. He was pushing a shopping cart when he spotted Leah in the produce section, sniffing melons. Her hair was down, and he experienced a familiar tightening in his gut at the sight of her. She moved with such an easy, feminine grace and he watched her for several seconds, remembering how good she felt in his arms, how sexy she was when her beautiful hair fanned over his chest, how utterly mesmerizing her lips were, how good it felt to have her in his arms.

She looked up and their gazes clashed, but within seconds she was smiling, and Sean thought how odd it was that the tension in his gut seeped away. She had an unusual cathartic effect on him, as though her presence was some kind of balm, made to soothe and make things seem right with the world. He'd never met anyone like her. And certainly never been involved with anyone who was more friend than lover, even though the sex was out of this world.

He pushed his cart forward and met her beside a table of beets. "Hey there."

"Hi. I'm just picking up a few things to make a pie," she said and pointed to her cart. "You know, for Thanksgiving."

Sean had almost forgotten about the holiday. He knew his mother was expecting him to attend the family celebration at Kieran's and of course he would show his face, but he knew he wasn't in the frame of mind to linger. The truth was, he'd had his fill of family gatherings in the last week.

"I won't be making pie," he said and grinned.

Her brows furrowed. "Aren't you seeing your family tomorrow?"

He nodded. "Yeah. I thought I'd pick up a gift basket from the deli section."

"You can't do that," she retorted. "I'll tell you what, come over tonight and I'll teach you how to make apple pie and you can take it tomorrow."

Sean grimaced. "I suck at baking."

"You're never too old to learn a new skill," she reminded him. "I think my dad is going to see a play at the local theater tonight with your mom."

Sean's gut twitched, and Leah noticed his darkening expression. "Don't get all thingy about it," she scolded. "They're friends. You should be happy about that."

"Friends like *we're* friends?" he remarked, tugging at his collar a little. "Anyway, I'd rather not think about it. It's my mom, remember."

"You're such a baby about some things," she said and laughed. "I'll see you tonight, about seven."

She headed off in the other direction, and Sean remained where he was for a moment, watching the gentle sway of her hips as she moved, thinking things he figured were a little too X-rated for the supermarket. When he got home a short while later, he put the groceries away and settled at the table with his laptop and cell phone. He had a few ideas on who to invite to Leah's show and began making arrangements.

At about ten to seven he grabbed a six-pack of cider and walked to Ivan's place. The dogs barked for a few seconds and then greeted him excitedly. He petted them both just as Leah appeared on the front veranda. It was a cold night, and she was dressed in jeans, a colorful tunic and bright purple moccasins.

"You look nice," he said as he followed her inside.

Sean passed her the cider and then quickly ditched his jacket before following her down the hall and into the kitchen. He grinned when he noticed how she had the bowls already lined up on the countertop. She flipped the tops of two cider bottles and placed the rest in the refrigerator.

"Ready for your baking lesson?" she asked and slid a bottle across the counter.

"Sure," he replied.

Half an hour later Sean admitted to himself that pie making wasn't nearly as bad an idea as he'd first thought. As usual, Leah was good company and patient as she explained the art of making pastry.

"Do you do this often?" he asked, smiling at the smear of flour on her nose.

She nodded. "I like to cook. I like being creative, I guess."

"When I lived in LA, there was an Italian place around the corner, and I used to order dinner to go at least three nights a week. Shameful." He tsked, then grinned.

She shook her head with mock dismay. "Preparing food is half the fun."

"Well," he said agreeably, "it's fun when you have company. By the way, Liam offered me a job today." He shrugged, not sure why he was telling her, since he had no intention of accepting the offer.

"Really?"

He briefly explained about Connie's maternity leave and how Liam wanted to step back a little from his workload. "Oh, and Kieran thinks I'm back in town because I'm a recovering drug addict."

She laughed loudly. "They don't know you very well, do they? Anyone can see that you're too vanilla to do drugs."

"What does that mean?"

"That your bad boy reputation is just a disguise for your Goody Two-shoes reality."

Sean's hands stilled and he stared at her. "My *what*?"

"I'm not fooled," she said and bumped her hip against his. "You like helping people. Like, hanging out with my dad, or helping me get over my fear of failure. Addicts aren't that selfless. Besides, I don't imagine you'd like being out of control. I've also noticed that you hardly drink, don't smoke and have no obvious vices."

"I sound near perfect."

She laughed again. "Hardly."

The camaraderie he experienced being with her

was humbling. And arousing. And confusing. "I'm sorry if I was a jerk yesterday. I don't mean to be."

"I know," she said and passed him a wooden spoon. "Some habits are heard to break. So, are you going to take Liam up on his offer?"

"Of course not," he replied. "I don't have any idea how to run a hotel."

Leah rose one speculative brow, motioned toward the lumps of pastry dough on the counter and shrugged. "I guess it's like anything—you could learn. And it is the O'Sullivan Hotel, and you are an O'Sullivan," she reminded him. "Just saying."

"He only offered because he thinks I need something to keep me occupied. I'm not interested in a pity offer."

She turned, resting one hip against the counter, and reached up to touch his face with her flour-smeared hands, turning his gaze toward her. "You don't think it could be because you're smart, successful, influential and have a stellar résumé?"

Sean's gut took a dive. Damn, the woman knew which buttons to push to make him *think*. "There's that near perfect thing again."

"I'm only saying," she said and dropped her hand, "that you shouldn't be suspicious of everyone's motives, particularly not your family's. It's well-known that Liam has really turned the hotel around in the last five years. It's something of an icon in this town and important to not only the dozens of people who work there, but also the rest of the community. Other businesses rely on it to bring tourist dollars into town. Don't underestimate the value of the hotel—without it, Cedar River wouldn't be flourishing, but would be just like so many other small towns around the state. I wouldn't be so quick to dismiss the idea, or what you could bring to it to ensure it continues to grow. Besides, who knows where it might lead. It doesn't mean you have to give up any other plans to get back to the music industry. And maybe Liam needs you, have you thought about that?"

Sean stared at her, mesmerized by the passion in her voice. "You know, you should run for mayor."

"Maybe I will one day," she replied. "You should at least consider it."

"I will," he said and nodded, grabbing her hands, forgetting the cooking lesson for a moment as he urged her closer. "I'd prefer to think about something else at the moment."

She laughed. "I know exactly what you're thinking about," she said as her hips came into contact with his.

Sean kissed her hotly, because he wanted to and mostly because he couldn't help himself. She kissed him back, and her arms settled around his waist. She felt so good in his arms.

"Leah," he whispered and trailed his mouth down her neck, lingering at the soft skin below her jaw because he couldn't get enough of the way she shivered when he kissed her there. "I don't think anyone has ever done what you do to my libido."

"Have you grown tired of long-legged blondes?"

"I like brunettes," he muttered, kissing her neck, "with purple and pink streaks. And great legs."

"And a flat chest?" she teased and dug her fingers into his back, urging him closer.

Sean pulled back a little and grasped her chin, gently forcing her to meet his gaze. "You are beautiful," he said, looking at her mouth because its lusciousness mesmerized him. "Don't you let anyone ever tell you different."

Sean watched as her eyes glittered, and then glistened. He hadn't expected tears, and they threw him, forming an ache deep in his chest, making him want to haul her closer and protect her from whatever it was that was upsetting her. The notion instantly stunned him. Had he ever experienced such an intense and overprotective reaction before? He couldn't recall, couldn't remember ever experiencing such a raw and powerful pull toward another human being.

It shocked him. Calmed him. Terrified him. And the idea that he was so at the mercy of his feelings made Sean want to simultaneously run *and* stay.

He wiped the tear that formed at the corner of her eye and dropped his forehead to hers. What could he say? *Let me stay? Let me make love to you? My arms feel empty when you're not in them?*

Sean shook off his thoughts. He couldn't get in any deeper. And yet he didn't know how to drag himself out of what he was feeling. And that meant he had to end it. Soon.

* * *

Leah sent Sean home not long before her dad returned, pushing the fabulously baked pie into his hands and accepting a long and delicious kiss before he left. It would have been easier to ask him to stay the night, or at least follow him back to his place and enjoy a long night of lovemaking. But…she had to keep her boundaries strong on occasion so he didn't see how much she craved him.

Or loved him.

It had been a startling revelation and one she wasn't entirely ready to admit, since it had crept up on her, sometimes even making her question her sanity. Because she had to be out of her mind to fall in love with a man like Sean—who'd made it clear he wasn't in the market for love or anything remotely resembling a relationship.

But she was in love with him, despite the futility that accompanied that love in her heart.

It was nothing like her feelings for Gary, or even Xavier. Gary had swooped in and used her attraction to confuse and manipulate her. And Xavier hadn't been much better. But there was nothing manipulative about Sean—he was forthright about their arrangement. They were friends who had sex. Falling in love with him was on her, not him. She certainly wasn't about to burden him with the news, not when he had so much of his own going on. Still, she knew she needed to take a step back, so sending him home after making pies was a step in that direction. Even if all she truly wanted was to fall into his arms and never leave.

Her father returned a little after ten, and she noticed how much happier he seemed lately and figured it had little to do with her moving back in, and everything to do with Gwen.

"You've been baking," he said and gestured to the pans drying on the draining board.

"We made pies for tomorrow."

His brow cocked. "We?"

She looked away for a moment, busying herself with drying dishes. "Sean came over."

Ivan's expression softened. "You've been spending a lot of time together."

She shrugged. "We're just friends, Dad, I told you."

"Are you sure that's all?"

Leah met her father's gaze and sighed. "You know that's not all. But it's complicated. He's not…emotionally available. I know what you're thinking," she added when she saw his expression shift. "Trust me to fall for the wrong guy, again."

"You think he's wrong for you?"

"Don't you?"

Ivan smiled. "You know I like Sean. But I don't like seeing you unhappy."

"I'm not, I promise. I know what I'm doing," she lied. "And Sean hasn't made any promises he can't keep. So, relax, Dad, I'm fine. I'll see you in the morning."

Leah headed for her bedroom and stared at the walls for an hour before she finally managed to fall asleep. When she woke up around seven o'clock, there was a light blanket of snow on the ground, and once she'd had breakfast and took the dogs for a short walk, she spent a few hours in the studio. After lunch she showered and changed and packed up a basket with the food she needed to take to the Triple C. She and Ivan headed off around two o'clock. There were half a dozen cars already parked in the driveway, and she quickly spotted her brother's SUV. She'd hardly spent any time with her niece and nephew in the last couple of weeks and knew she needed to remedy that. Leah admired Annie's resolve. She wasn't prepared to settle for less than all of David's love, and gave him the time he needed to come to his senses and realize Annie was the love of his life.

Leah sighed, wondering if she'd ever find that kind of love.

Mitch greeted them by the door and ushered them inside. Her dad remained in the foyer with him when Tess approached with Charlie, and Leah waved hellos all around before she headed down the hall. The kitchen was also bursting with Culhanes, including Ellie and Grant. She waved another hello as she spotted David by the counter, chatting to Mrs. Bailey, Mitch and Tess's housekeeper. When David saw her, he grinned broadly and quickly came across the room and enveloped her in an affectionate hug.

"Hey there, kid," he said and smiled. "Where's Dad?"

"With Mitch and Tess."

"It's so good to see you. It feels like forever."

She knew what he meant, even though they'd seen each other at the wedding five days earlier, she hadn't had much opportunity to talk. "When are you guys leaving for your honeymoon?" she asked, hugging him back, and then placed the basket on the countertop.

"Saturday," he replied and smiled. "You know the kids are coming, right? Annie insisted. And Mittie is coming, too, so we have a sitter."

"A romantic honeymoon in Hawaii," she teased. "With two kids and a grandmother."

"I know," he said and sighed, looping an arm over her shoulder. "But Annie wanted them to come along, and since I can't refuse my beautiful wife anything, I agreed."

They walked down the hallway and into the front living room. Jasper and Scarlett rushed toward her, and she hugged them. "I made your favorite Thanksgiving cookies," she said and ruffled their hair. "They're in the kitchen. Ask Mrs. Bailey to get them from the basket."

The kids hurried off with an excited cheer, and she sat down on one of the sofas beside her brother. Annie was by the window, talking with Jake and Abby, and she spotted Hank and Joss out on the veranda. As much as she loved her family and knew she was loved in return, Leah experienced an unusual and acute sense of disconnect in that moment and wasn't sure why.

"So," David said in his sternest big brother voice, "since we didn't get a chance to discuss this at the wedding—what's the deal with you and O'Sullivan?"

Of course she'd been expecting the conversation. David was as overprotective as any normal older brother. "We're friends."

"You brought him to the wedding," David reminded her. "And slow danced."

Heat crawled up her neck. "You saw that?"

David nodded. "Everyone saw that. Are you dating him?"

"No comment."

He scowled. "Just be careful. You know he's got a bad reputation when it comes to women."

Leah made an impatient sound. "I know that he's lived in California for the last ten years, so no one would really know what he did or didn't do," she said, feeling hotly defensive. "And it's not like you to judge people."

"Whoa," David said and held up a hand. "I wasn't attacking him. I hardly know the guy, but I'm concerned about you."

"No need to be," she retorted. "I'm doing great. I'm working on several new metalwork designs, and I'm happy to report that the piece I did for the hotel is now in place. In fact, I'm about to have a showing at the gallery in town."

"You are?"

If anyone knew about her polarizing insecurity, it was David. "I am. I'll be sure to send you an invitation."

"How did this come about?"

She quickly explained how Gwen had made the offer and how Sean was supporting the idea and helping with the planning. "It's all happening pretty fast, which is probably for the best because it means I won't have time to talk myself out of it."

"Sounds like O'Sullivan is making all your dreams come true."

She noticed the seed of suspicion in her brother's expression and quickly reassured him. "He's used to working with creative types like me," she said and grinned. "And he's amazingly supportive. I couldn't ask for a better friend."

David sat back in the sofa and stared at her. "I see."

"What does that mean?"

"You're in love with him."

Her cheeks burned. "So what if I am," she said defensively and then let out a heavy sigh.

"You've been in love before," he reminded her.

"I know," she admitted. "But maybe this time I'm hoping it will be different," she said and got to her feet. She didn't want to argue with her brother. In fact, all she wanted to do was leave and get some fresh air. Leah excused herself and left the room, finding a little solace on one corner of the veranda. She sat down on a love seat just as her cell pinged.

She pulled the phone from her pocket and checked the message, smiling when she recognized Sean's number.

I've been here under two hours and I've already had enough of all this familial closeness and happy coupledom. You?

She nodded to herself and quickly replied.

I hear you. How did the pie go down?

He replied instantly.

Highlight of the day. Although I was teased by my brothers for baking. They asked if I was taking up knitting next.

He added a humorous emoji that made her laugh out loud.

You're in luck. I know how to knit. Would you like to go horseback riding tomorrow?

His response was immediate.

Not really. But I would like to cook you dinner Saturday night. Seven o'clock?

Her heart skipped a beat.

That sounds good.

He finished the conversation with a thumbs-up emoji, and Leah stuffed the cell back into her pocket. She could hear laugher from inside the house, but remained where she was, thinking about Sean, finding comfort in the knowledge he was feeling as out of place as she was.

She'd never believed in soul mates or kindred spirits, but knowing Sean had changed all that. Perhaps she should summon the courage and lay out her feelings, play her hand and see where the cards fell. What did she have to lose?

Everything...

Her pride *and* her heart.

She just didn't know if she had the courage to take such a leap of faith.

Chapter Ten

Sean was so out of sorts he felt as though his collar was strangling him. For one, there was so much chatter around the Thanksgiving dinner table, it all merged into one long drone that sounded more like white noise than conversation. Several times he asked people to repeat themselves and then wondered if they noticed.

The truth was, he was lonely.

Lonely for Leah. She understood him. She knew the struggles he was facing. She had his back. His family, on the other hand, was all lively and cheerful and clearly delighted to be in each other's company. And it was weird, seeing his father at one end of the table with his wife Kathleen, and his mother at the other end of the table. And it was also weird looking at Jonah and seeing how his half brother had parents who were now together, while Sean's parents were apart. He'd grown up thinking his folks had a happy marriage, but now suspected that wasn't exactly the case. True, things were strained after Liz died, but deep down he knew things were fractured before that. Maybe they'd always been bad, but he'd been too blind to see it. Maybe his father had married the wrong woman from the beginning and should have been with Kathleen all along.

What did he know about true love or marriage?

Not a damned thing.

He'd spent the last decade avoiding anything that looked like commitment or intimacy. In the last few years, he'd watched his brothers—all three of them—fall in love and get married and hadn't experienced one spark of envy or longing.

Except for right now.

Because despite the fact that he was a part of the family surrounding him, he felt…disconnected. His own doing, he figured. Since Liz's death he pulled back from everyone, even if he hadn't recognized it at the time. And then the whole thing with Jonah had blown up in their faces and he'd pulled away even further. So he had no one to blame for the disconnection he was experiencing, except himself. He knew it. But didn't know how to fix it. And worse, didn't know if he wanted it fixed.

Once the meal was over, he took off for the living room and hung out with Johnny and Marco for a while. The boys had new gaming consoles and were eager to show them off. It was funny, he thought, how he'd become the *cool* uncle. He didn't feel particularly cool. He didn't feel anything. Except perhaps bored with himself. Working on the details for Leah's art showing had proven something to himself he wasn't quite ready to acknowledge—he needed to work.

"You planning on hiding out here for the rest of the day?"

It was Will's voice he heard from the doorway, although only barely. He looked up and saw his friend, who regularly joined the clan for the holidays as Will's mother and Gwen had been the closest of friends for decades. Will's mom had passed away a few years earlier, but his friend still stopped by and kept in touch with the family and had been invited for the holiday this year. Kieran was with him, and the pair came into the room and sat opposite in a couple of occasional chairs.

"So," Kieran said and grinned. "Where's your girlfriend today?"

He couldn't even summon impatience. "Leah's not my girlfriend."

"Sure she is," Kieran contradicted, still grinning. "Mom said the pair of you are inseparable."

His gut twitched. "A gross exaggeration."

"Going to family functions together," Kieran said and ticked off a finger to make the point. "Painting your house together." Another tick. "Spending alone time together." One more tick. "And I'll bet she had something to do with that pie you say you baked. That, I hate to tell you, is a girlfriend."

"He's right," Will agreed and laughed. "You've so got a girlfriend."

"You're wrong."

"Really?" Kieran queried. "So, when are you seeing her again?"

"Saturday," he said and then wished he hadn't. "It's just a casual dinner."

Will laughed. "It's a date. All that's left is for you to buy a ring and pop the question."

Sean knew they were teasing, but he didn't like it. He didn't want anyone speculating about his relationship with Leah. Not that they were in a *relationship*. But he still didn't appreciate gossip or innuendo.

He glared at them. "Stay out of it."

He saw them say something to one another, and that amplified his feeling of exclusion and fueled his irritation. When Kieran spoke again, he was frowning a little.

"Ignoring it won't make it go away."

Sean strained to hear him. "What?"

"The fact that you ignored Jonah all through dinner. I know he's not perfect," Kieran said with an impatient sigh, "but neither are you. And he's trying, so maybe you could meet him halfway."

Halfway? Sean wasn't even sure what that meant. And he hadn't deliberately set out to ignore anyone during dinner. If Jonah was speaking to him, he wasn't aware of it. And he knew the moment he'd been dreading for months was suddenly staring him in the face.

"I've gotta get another piece of that pie," Will said, looking at Kieran before rounding up Marco and Johnny. Sean found himself alone with Kieran—and knew what was coming.

"What?" he demanded.

"Exactly," Kieran said, getting to his feet and quickly sitting beside him on the couch. "What's going on? And don't tell me to back off. I'm asking you as your brother, goddammit, not as a doctor."

Sean opened his mouth to speak, then clamped his lips together. He'd never been the type of man who opened up or trusted easily, not even with his own family. Stubborn, Leah had called him. She'd also said it was a flaw. And deep down, he knew she was right.

He inhaled sharply. "Sensorineural hearing loss."

Kieran frowned. "What?"

"I imagine you've heard of it?"

His brother nodded. "Of course." Comprehension flashed across his face. "Sean, have you—"

"I was diagnosed about a year ago," he said flatly. "I noticed my hearing changing a few years back. Constant tinnitus, other things like that. At first I thought I was imagining it, so I ignored it. Then I blamed the equipment in the studio. Then I thought it was some kind of middle ear infection. You name it, I blamed it, until it became obvious there was a problem and I finally got tested. It's still deteriorating at this stage."

Kieran looked at him. "You know it's irreversible?"

He nodded. "Eventually, I'll be deaf."

"So this is why you came back?" Kieran asked bluntly. "Because of your diagnosis?"

"Well…yeah."

His brother sighed. "Is that why you sold your studio? Because you were worried you couldn't do the job? If that's the case, it doesn't sound like you. I mean, I've never known you to quit something."

He knew Kieran was only trying to get him to open up, to try to understand his decisions. The trouble was, Sean didn't feel like laying his feelings on the line. "It was just timing and opportunity."

Kieran didn't looked convinced, but nodded. "Have you considered hearing aids? What about learning ASL? Have you thought about working on this? I think we have a program—"

"It's an option," he replied, cutting his brother off. "I'm not…" Suddenly, he just couldn't say it again. Not to his brother.

"Ready?" Keiran suggested. "Understandable. It's a big adjustment, but I'm confident you'll get through it. You get through everything, Sean." He put a hand on his brother's shoulder, his touch and his tone gentle, yet reassuring. "I mean it. And no matter what, we are always going to be here for you."

Sean shrugged. "I guess my misspent youth listening to all that loud music caught up with me," he added and managed a grin. "But I'm seeing a specialist in Rapid City. I'm working on it, Kieran."

Kieran rolled his eyes, then turned serious again. "Thank you for telling me."

Sean's throat tightened. "You won't say anything to Mom and Dad?"

"No," Kieran replied. "But *you* should."

He sighed heavily. "You know how Mom will get. She worries about everything and I don't want to add to that. And all Dad and I seem to do these days is argue."

Kieran didn't disagree and they spent a few more minutes talking before he excused himself and bailed.

Once he'd said a brief goodbye to his parents, he took off for home. The drive through town was quiet, and few cars were on the road. He turned off and headed down his driveway. And then got an unexpected surprise. Leah was sitting on the steps, bundled up in a coat, hat and boots.

Sean didn't bother parking in the garage, instead pulling up outside the house. She didn't move when he got out of the car and approached her, but she met his gaze and he watched her throat convulse as she drew in a long breath. Sean's ribs tightened, and he didn't do anything for a moment but simply look at her, absorbing the lovely angles of her face, her stunning hair, her generous mouth and her vulnerable expression.

"What's wrong?" he asked.

"Nothing...now."

His insides contracted even further, and he held out his hand. "Come here."

She took his hand and he urged her to her feet, quickly wrapping his arms around her. "I've had an average day," she admitted and sighed. "You?"

"About the same," he replied.

"What happened?"

He sighed. "I told Kieran about my diagnosis."

She touched his face. "I'm glad. That's a big first step."

"Yeah," he agreed. "I think he wanted to dig deep, you know, get me to talk about selling the business and coming back."

"And you couldn't?"

"I didn't want to sound like a spoiled brat," he said, echoing the accusation his father had thrown at him several days earlier. Even though it was about something else, Sean was smart enough to see the connection in his behavior. "Because the truth is, I *could* have stuck it out. I could have worked around it. I could have made modifications to the studio. I could have done a whole lot of things. But I didn't because I was angry," he admitted, his arms tightening around her. "I was pissed off that this had happened to me and went with my original reaction—which was to say to hell with it and sell up before anyone figured it out."

It was the first time he'd really said the words. The first time he'd allowed himself to *feel* them. And he felt like such a coward. Like he'd given in. *Given up*. On everything he had. On everything he *was*.

"You're too hard on yourself," she said, knowing him so well it was terrifying.

"Maybe," he said. "But I did use it as an excuse to give up."

"I don't think so, Sean," she said gently. "I think that maybe it was more like a *reason* for you to come home."

"Thank you, Leah," he said. "You always make me see a different side of things."

She dropped her head onto his chest and shuddered, and he held her tighter, absorbing the warmth of her through to his bones. Finally she lifted her head and turned her face upward. "Sean," she said, speaking clearly. "Would you make love to me?"

His body clenched with a heavy ache. "I've been wanting to do that all day."

They walked up the stairs and then inside, and without another word they headed for his bedroom. It was almost cathartic the way they removed one another's clothes, and her touch was like a tonic. Every stroke, each gentle touch of her fingertips was calming and created an almost cosmic shift in his soul. He kissed her deeply and she kissed him back. He caressed her with a kind of reverence he'd never experienced before, but was so caught up in the moment, in the passion they shared, he didn't dare to wonder why her touch was like no other. She came apart in his arms, saying his name over and over like a chant, and once birth control was in place, Sean rolled onto his back and took her with him, placing his hands on her hips, urging her into a primal, erotic rhythm that shattered his control and made him groan with pleasure. There was something almost pagan about the way she looked as she ground her hips against him, her beautiful wanton hair tumbling over her shoulders, her head thrown back, exposing her long smooth neck. Her nipples were hard peaks and he longed to put his mouth there, to tease the pebbled pink flesh with his tongue, and the mental image undid him. He matched her rhythm, grinding against her, feeling her body shudder, taking him on a wild ride that was mind-blowing in its intensity as release claimed him. He couldn't think. Couldn't do anything other than feel. He'd had great sex in the past—but nothing like this. He wasn't used to losing his mind. She collapsed against him, kissing him long and hard, her tongue in his mouth even though they were both panting and breathless. But he didn't care. He didn't want the feeling to end. Didn't want to lose the connection and unbridled intimacy of their joining.

"Holy Mother of God," he muttered against her mouth before she moved her lips and began kissing his neck. "That was incredible."

She pulled back and looked into his eyes. "We do seem to get this right."

"I'm not exaggerating," he said and ran his hands down her hips and thighs and then back up, looping them around her waist. "My brain is addled. I always thought that it was a myth."

"What was a myth?"

"The perfect moment," he replied, kissing her shoulder. "You know, truly sensational sex."

"Well, you have more to compare it to than me," she said and smiled.

"Not as many as you might think," he said and touched her face. "So, like I said," he whispered, trailing his mouth up her collarbone. "Perfect."

They stayed in bed for a while, touching and making out, talking about nothing in particular and avoiding discussing the day they'd had. He knew she was unhappy, knew she'd somehow had a bad day and needed something from him. Solace, he thought vaguely, feeling the passion return as she trailed kisses down his chest and belly. Perhaps that's what they were to one another? Maybe that's why they had connected. Even though she did things to his libido he hadn't imagined possible, there was some other connection that drew them together. Kinship. Friendship. *Soulship*—if there was such a thing.

It was after nine when they dragged themselves from bed, had a shower and afterward snuggled on the couch and watched television. She wore a baggy pair of his sweats, the hems rolled up to her ankles and wrists, and looked as sexy as hell.

"Want to tell me about it?" he asked, tracing his fingertips along one bare foot.

"About my crappy day?" she remarked, looking at him. "Not really. And it wasn't so bad...just a lot people in one place who think they know me and can tell me how to live my life."

"Ah," he said and smiled. "I take it big brother had something to say?"

She shrugged. "David was simply being David. Overprotective and opinionated. Although he *was* surprised when I told him about the art show. I'm sure he believed I'd never do it again after the last time."

"You'll be fine," he assured her, seeing doubt cloud her expression. "And I'm certain it will be successful."

Her gaze narrowed. "But how can you be sure?"

"Instinct," he replied. "Experience. You're in good hands."

She grabbed his fingers and squeezed them. "I know."

Something uncurled in his chest, a feeling he wasn't accustomed to. "Leah, you know I like the time we spend together." He saw her nod, and also saw the uncertainty in her expression. "But I'm not ready for anything serious—like a relationship."

"I know that."

Guilt pitched in his chest. She was so damned

agreeable. He should have been reassured, but wasn't. "It's only that we've talked about this...you know...about us. You know I'm not looking for anything permanent right now."

She pulled her hand away. "Are you truly that egotistical?"

He stilled. "It's not ego, it's honesty."

"You mean it's okay to be hurtful if you're doing it with the best intentions?"

"I don't mean to hurt you," he insisted and swung his legs off the couch. "If I have, then I'm sorry. But I thought you understood what this was about."

"I do," she said hotly. "But your constant need to remind me is a little tiring, and frankly unnecessary. I know what you want, Sean. I know you're not interested in commitment or a relationship. I know you want to keep this casual. So then *keep* it casual," she said and got to her feet. "And stop implying that *I* want something else."

"Don't you?" he asked bluntly.

"What *I* want isn't the issue," she replied. "You know what I think—I think you keep bringing this up because it gives you an easy escape clause. Well, you don't need one. If you want to end this, then end it."

His insides lurched. "I don't want to end it, Leah. I just don't want to hurt you."

"Then don't," she said. "I'm not fragile, Sean. I've been hurt in the past and managed to pull through it. I'm not about to fall apart at the idea of breaking up with you—since we're not really dating anyway. Friends with benefits, remember?"

He didn't like the way that sounded. Stupid. Some modern, meaningless term for a connection that went deeper than friendship. But he wasn't about to admit such a thing. It was better she believed he was disinterested in anything more, just as she was. Anyhow, that was the truth. He wasn't the *relationship* kind of guy. Never had been. But he'd never been with a woman like Leah, either. He was drawn to her lack of artifice; the way she wore her jeans and flowing tops; the way she swayed when she walked; to her luscious mouth and the lovely colors of her hair; and the way it felt so damned good threaded between his fingers or trailing over his chest.

"Did you want to know why I came here this afternoon?" she asked, her voice quiet, but oddly, he could hear every word. "Because I wanted a friend, not only a lover. And not a boyfriend, Sean, if that's what's worrying you."

But he was worried. For her. For them. And for himself.

Leah wasn't sure how she found the strength to stay with him on Thanksgiving night. But staying seemed the lesser of two evils. If she left, he would have more questions, more attempts at pacifying her with words about not wanting to hurt her, or platitudes about what he couldn't give her. In the end, she headed back to his bedroom and went to sleep.

Or at least pretended to. He didn't join her until well after midnight, and by then she was lying on her side, controlling her breathing, trying to look as though she was sleeping. He didn't disturb her, didn't try to hold her, didn't do anything other than roll over, plump out a pillow and let out a long sigh.

She got up early, dressed quickly and left without saying goodbye to him as he was still dozing. She headed home, and as always, the dogs were waiting for her by the back door and her father was already in the kitchen.

"Morning," Ivan said and looked up from his tea and crossword puzzle.

Leah sat down opposite her father, placed her elbows on the table and let out a long breath. "David thinks I'm in love with Sean."

"And are you?" Ivan queried and sipped his tea.

She shrugged. "There's not much point in loving a man who doesn't believe in love."

"Are you sure that's how he feels?"

Heat burned her eyes. "You know him, Dad... Sean isn't exactly emotionally accessible."

"Are *you*?"

She met his worried gaze. "Maybe not," she said and got to her feet, glancing at the clock on the wall. "Don't forget the physiotherapist is coming this morning," she reminded him. It had taken some effort getting her father to agree to in-house visits by the physical therapist, but finally he'd given in to her nagging. It meant he didn't have to travel into town and could have more regular sessions. "If you don't need me for anything, I promised Ellie I'd go riding with her this morning. Apparently Chico needs some exercise."

He father nodded. "You're fond of that animal, aren't you?"

"Yes."

"I'd be happy to give you the money to buy him," Ivan said quietly. "Even though I know Mitch has offered the horse to you free of charge."

Leah inhaled heavily. "And I'll tell you exactly what I said to Mitch—thank you, but no. I won't allow you to dip into your savings, and I won't take charity from my cousin."

"David would give you the money in a heartbeat," Ivan remarked.

"I know," she said. "Which is exactly why I would never take it. I do have my pride, Dad, regardless of what you all think. Xavier may have cleaned out my bank account, but that doesn't mean I'd resort to handouts from relatives. I'm going to get changed, and then I'll see you later."

She was at the Triple C within the hour and met Ellie by the stable. Chico was also waiting for her, stamping an impatient foot as she tacked him up and snorting when she tightened the cinch. They went for a long ride along the fence perimeter, and Leah was happy for the chance to spend time with Chico and not think about everything else. Or someone else in particular. When they returned, it was close to lunchtime and the weather had begun to turn. They hitched the horses on the rail near the corral with the plan to give them a solid brush down.

"Chico behaved well, but he's been in a mood this week," Ellie said and stood beside her. "He's the type of horse that needs work every couple of days, and I don't have time to ride both him and Valiant," she said and hooked a thumb in the direction of her big gelding. "Besides, Chico only likes you."

Leah stroked the animal's face. "He has impeccable taste," she said and grinned.

"You left the party early yesterday," Ellie said, swiftly changing the subject. "Want to talk about it?"

Leah grabbed the bridle and looped the reins of Chico's neck as she eased the bit from his mouth. "Not especially."

"You were talking with David," Ellie commented. "And then you bailed. I get it, you know—remember, I have *five* brothers."

Leah gave a brittle laugh. If anyone knew about being suffocated by family advice, it was Ellie. Her cousin had also had her fair share of disastrous relationships.

"Do you think you'll ever get married?"

Ellie made a face. "Well, since I haven't had a date in months, it doesn't seem likely at this rate. Particularly not with any or all of my brothers watching me like a hawk. And honestly, I'm so busy with studying and this ranch, I don't think I could fit anyone into my life at this point. If I did, he would have to be a saint."

"No such thing."

"I can dream," Ellie said and made a swoony face. "It's a pity all the O'Sullivan boys are taken."

Leah knew her cousin was teasing and tried to remain in good humor. "You are so off the mark."

"Sure I am," Ellie said and grinned. "That's why there's a red Ferrari coming up the driveway as we speak."

She snapped her head around. Sure enough, there *was* a red Ferrari. "It could be anyone."

Ellie laughed. "Really? That car in this town—not a chance. I'm going to take Valiant back to his stall."

Her cousin disappeared into the stables, and Leah had resumed untacking Chico as the car pulled up. Sean quickly got out. Dressed in jeans, a white shirt, a black leather jacket and sunglasses, he looked like a male model advertising a luxury sports car. He approached wordlessly, coming to stand about five feet away. Chico snorted and she glanced toward Sean, waiting for him to speak.

"You left without saying goodbye this morning."

She turned, conscious of her habit of facing him when she spoke. "You were sleeping. How did you know I was here?"

"You told me," he replied, coming closer, taking off the sunglasses.

"I don't remember doing that."

"You asked me if I wanted to go riding this morning," he reminded her. "I assumed that meant you'd be here. Nice horse."

She patted Chico's neck. "I adore him. He makes my heart happy."

"And yet you won't make him your own, correct?"

"Charity," she stated. "Mitch is simply being overly generous. And I won't allow my father to pay for him. Or my brother. I do have some pride."

"I'd say you have bucketloads of it," he remarked. "Do you think you can put it aside to embrace an opportunity brought about by a friend?"

She was instantly suspicious. "What friend?"

"You have a meeting with Vance Beaumont on Tuesday."

Leah frowned. "Who's that?"

"The owner of one of the largest hotels and casinos in Las Vegas."

Leah blinked and then shook her head. "I don't understand what that means. You want me to go to Vegas?"

"Vance owes me a favor," he said and shrugged. "A few years ago his sister had aspirations to be a singer. I gave her shot."

"Lola Beaumont?" she asked quickly. "The hip-hop star?"

He nodded. "Yes. Vance is redesigning his casino and needs a centerpiece for the foyer. I sent him a picture of what you did for Liam, and he was impressed. I've booked our flights, and we leave from Rapid City airport at nine twenty Tuesday morning."

Leah's head spun. "I couldn't possibly."

"Why not?" he asked. "Somewhere else you need to be on Tuesday?"

"Yes," she told him. "Here. Home. With my dad. That's why I moved back in, to be close."

"You weren't there last night," he reminded her. "Or any of the other nights you've spent in my bed."

"I can't," she insisted. "I don't have my portfolio ready and I—"

"Don't be a chicken, Leah," he challenged. "You can do this."

"What's in it for you?" she asked, annoyed that he'd made assumptions about what she wanted.

"A trip to Vegas. I get to hang out with you. Stay at a fancy hotel. Take your pick."

"I really have become quite the pet project for you, haven't I?" she asked shrilly, not giving a damn if he heard her complaints or not. "No doubt this sudden interest in my failing career is a way to alleviate your boredom."

"It's not that," he assured her, although she didn't believe him. "This would be quite the coup, particularly since it's timed right before your showing. Vance wants to meet you and see if you can share his vision for something unique and creative. This is a good thing, Leah…don't let pride or fear stop you from taking all you deserve."

She faced him directly, speaking clearly so he understood every word. "Nice speech. You really are good at this, aren't you—I'll bet you spent the last

decade stroking the egos of vulnerable and uncon-
fident artists."

"When I needed to."

She made a scoffing sound. "No sweet wonder
you were so successful. Did you also sweeten the
offer with a tumble in the sack with Lola Beaumont?"

He laughed. "Get real. She was sixteen, so definitely not. Stop being a coward."

"That's rich, coming from you," she said, both
brows up. "You can't even tell your parents the truth
about why you moved back to Cedar River."

His expression darkened, and he slipped the sunglasses back onto his face. "It's an opportunity, Leah.
If you don't want to take it, that's fine. I'll see you
tomorrow night, at seven."

She shook her head. "Forget it. I don't want to
spend any more time with you."

"Sure you do," he drawled. "See you then."

Leah was still fuming long after his car had gen-
erated a cloud of dust as it retreated down the driveway. She pulled off Chico's saddle and hitched it on
her hip, calling for one of the stable hands. The youth
quickly came over from the corral and took the saddle, and she led Chico back into his stall. Ellie was
still there with Valiant and came out just as Leah
was bolting the stall door.

"That was a short visit," her cousin remarked.

Leah spent exactly one minute explaining the situation, and Ellie quickly formed an opinion.

"Wow, that's huge, Leah! What a fabulous opportunity."

"Ha," she scoffed. "It's ridiculous. How can I possibly go? David will be in Hawaii, and I can't leave Dad alone and I—"

"I'll stay with Uncle Ivan," Ellie said quickly. "You have to go, Leah. This could be career altering."

"It's too much," she protested. "What if this Vance person hates my style and—"

"Then you have a romantic getaway with a hot guy and have some fun."

It sounded simple. Too simple. And Leah wasn't used to simple. She was used to being taken for a fool when it came to mixing relationships and her career. And she had no proof that this would turn out any different.

"I can't do it," she said. "The last time I trusted a man with my career it almost destroyed me. I'm not sure I could take another disappointment."

"Do you really think Sean would take advantage of you the way Gary or Xavier did?" Ellie asked earnestly. "I mean, he seems like a straight up, honest kind of guy."

"But how do I know?"

Ellie squeezed her arm. "I guess you don't. But everyone is a risk, Leah. It's simply a matter of how much risk you're willing to take."

"That's just it," she said and sighed heavily. "I don't know if it's worth it."

"If Sean's worth it, you mean?" Ellie asked and smiled. "Well, isn't this your chance to find out?"

Sure it was. But she still didn't know if she had the courage.

Because she had so much to lose.

Chapter Eleven

Leah had never been to Vegas before. But she had to admit, the lights, the strip, the noise, the energy that seemed to throb like a pulse was somehow mesmerizing. Sean, she suspected, had been there many times, because while she couldn't take her eyes off everything that whizzed by even in the daylight, he was sitting in the backseat of the rented limo, clicking keys on a laptop and not appearing even remotely interested in their surroundings. But he looked good, dressed in a gray suit, with a pale blue shirt and darker blue tie. Leah had dressed up, too, in a black pantsuit she knew flattered her figure, which she teamed with a crisp, white, wide-collared shirt and dressy boots.

"How many times have you been here?" she asked as she grabbed his arm to get his attention.

"A few," he replied. "Vance throws a good party."

"I guess you've met a lot of famous people?"

His mouth flattened for a second, and then he grinned. "A few."

"Like who?"

He exhaled and then rattled off the names of several celebrities, and it was an impressive list that made her feel stupidly insignificant.

"Are famous people as self-absorbed as the tabloids insinuate?"

"Some are," he replied. "But then, I've met some not so famous people who are equally as self-absorbed. I think it's the character, not the career."

It was Tuesday. She hadn't seen him since he'd made her dinner on Saturday night—where he hadn't repeated his invitation to meet Vance Beaumont. And she knew his play. He was allowing her to make her own decision in her own time. Because as she was discovering, Sean O'Sullivan was very good at getting people to do what he wanted. She talked the idea over with Ivan, and after some serious soul-searching, had decided to take a chance. She didn't stay Saturday night and he hadn't insisted. He'd picked her up that morning, and they had driven to Rapid City and caught their flight.

The Beaumont Hotel and casino was huge and imposing, and as she walked through the foyer about twenty minutes later, Leah's mind ticked over with possibilities. They met with Vance around two o'clock, and he gave them a tour. He was a tall, good-looking man in his late thirties, and she learned he'd inherited the hotel from his uncle. She did notice how Sean held on to her hand as they walked, and it was obvious that they were more than simple friends, although that was how he'd introduced her to the other man. They had a light lunch afterward in Vance's private rooms, and he suggested she work up a few ideas. He said the commission was hers and threw out a number that was way more than she'd expected.

"Not enough," Sean said as he placed his fork on the plate. "It's at least a three-month investment for Leah. Try adding about thirty percent onto that figure."

Leah almost kneed him under the table.

Vance did so without batting an eyelid. "Better?"

Sean nodded and looked at Leah. "You happy with that, Leah?"

"Ah…yeah."

"You'll get a contract drawn up?" Sean asked.

Vance nodded, and the negotiations were soon over. They left not long after and checked in to their suite. The huge king-size bed was hard to miss in the bedroom, and the view from the balcony was sublime.

"Wait until tonight," he said and moved up behind her by the balcony door. "The lights look incredible."

Leah turned around to face him. "How much does this suite cost? And the airplane tickets? And the limo? I'm only asking because I intend to pay you back."

"Stop worrying about money."

"That's easy to say when you have loads of it," she retorted. "And exactly what I would expect from an O'Sullivan."

Sean reached out and cupped her cheek. "I'm sorry I'm rich."

Leah saw the amusement in his eyes. "No, you're not. And I don't resent you your success, by the way, because I know you worked hard to get it. And since when did you set yourself up as my financial negotiator?"

"Since I'm better at it than you," he replied and urged her closer, nuzzling the sensitive spot below her jaw. "By the way, how much did my brother pay you for that piece you did for the hotel?"

She stated the price and then heard him curse. "I thought it was generous at the time."

He cursed again, still kissing her. "Liam's generous when it suits him, particularly when it comes to charity, but not so much when it comes to business. That's why he's the richest man in town, I guess." She heard him smile against her skin. "Well, second richest."

Leah grasped his shoulders and pulled back, meeting his gaze. "You do know I'm not your friend because of your money, right?"

"Of course I know. You're about the most scrupulous person I have ever met."

It was a lovely compliment. "What is it about money that makes people act so badly? I mean, Xavier stole my savings without it being even a blip on his conscience. I'll never understand that behavior."

"Me, either," he said and led her inside the room. "It's something of a paradox—people with money often behave badly, just as people without it do the same. There's no magic fix for badness, Leah. It's a learned behavior. But when money is valued above everything else, either the best or the worst of ourselves comes out."

"How did you do it?" she asked as they sat down. "How did you retain your ethics and sense of what was right and wrong."

"You mean, in big bad Hollywood?" He shrugged. "I guess, despite my resistance, I'm my father's son. Whatever J.D.'s flaws, he always insisted that a man was only ever as good as his word. Of course, at the time I didn't know he had a secret family tucked away in Portland," he said and shrugged again. "But you get what I mean."

She nodded. "I think your dad made the best of a hard situation. Like your mom is doing now, you know, staying civil, being generous with herself, even though it must hurt her to see J.D. and Kathleen married and clearly very much in love."

"I really want to hate Jonah," he admitted, swallowing hard.

Leah squeezed his hand, feeling so much love for him she could barely draw breath. "I know."

"But it's hard to hate someone who is…"

"So much like you?" she said, finishing his sentence. "And his father's son," she added, repeating the words he'd used only moments before. "As *you* are. I think you find it hard because hating someone isn't in your DNA. You have parents who raised you to be a good person. So be that best version of yourself and forgive your dad for being…human. For having weakness. For falling in love. And forgive Jonah, too…because he didn't ask to be born into your family. But he is your brother, he *is* family, and family should be treasured. Besides, you and Jonah are practically the same age, so he could be your friend as well as your sibling. Don't let your disappointment with your father cloud what could be a rewarding relationship."

He chuckled humorlessly. "It's terrifying how well you know me."

"Is it?" she countered, meeting his suddenly unsteady gaze.

He nodded soberly and drew her hand to his lips, kissing her knuckles. "How about we take a shower, get dressed and I'll show you my favorite places in town? Or if you like, we could spend some time downstairs playing blackjack?"

"I'm not much of a gambler," she admitted. "Seems like a waste of money to me."

"It might be fun," he said her and dragged her

to her feet. "We can stick to a one-hundred-dollar kitty, so your frugal sensibilities aren't challenged too much."

"I'm not frugal," she declared.

He laughed softly. "Honey, you turn scrap metal into pieces of artwork and sew patches on the worn-out places of your jeans."

"That's being fashion forward," she retorted.

"Although I must say," he added, running his hands down her back and bottom, "you look like the picture of professionalism in that suit. And as sexy as hell."

She giggled, feeling foolishly wonderful and free. They were away from Cedar River. Away from prying eyes. Away from the all the things that put their relationship in the *too hard* basket. And even though it was only for twenty-four hours, she could be with him and love him and pretend that they lived in a couple bubble.

Over the next few hours, Leah had so much fun she couldn't recall a time when she'd laughed so much, been kissed so often and wasted so much money. Well, she actually won a little at the roulette table, and Sean was amazingly generous. He stayed by her side while she played and then afterward they had dinner in one of the restaurants. He ordered champagne, Leah ate the most decadent lobster ravioli and once their empty dessert plates were taken away, they headed back to their suite and Sean made love to her. It was sweeter, more intense than any she'd ever known. It was touch that transcended the physical, and she couldn't stop the tears that burned her eyes, or the way her pulses raced, or the way her heart ached. And the words she'd kept inside came rushing out, bulldozing over protests, finding a voice even though she knew she was setting herself up for heartbreak.

"I love you, Sean."

He didn't reply. Didn't say a word, and she wondered if he'd heard her. But he kissed her, long and slow and deep, and for a while everything else was forgotten except the blinding passion that existed between them.

When Leah rolled out of bed the next morning, it was a little before eight o'clock. The space beside her was empty, the sheets cool, and she sat up and slipped on a robe, looking at the discarded clothes on the floor—his suit, her little black dress, the high heels she'd only worn once before. She padded out into the main room and saw a breakfast cart. But no Sean.

Maybe he's left.

It wouldn't surprise her, considering she'd broken all the rules and admitted she loved him. *So much for friends with benefits.* She was such a fraud. And now he knew as much.

She spotted him on the balcony, sitting at the small table, a cup of coffee in front of him. She approached, saying his name as she moved beside him, and he turned his head to meet her gaze.

"You let me sleep."

He was fully dressed, in dark jeans, a pale gray shirt and boots. "You seemed to need it."

Leah moved around and faced him. "Everything okay?"

He nodded and then dropped his gaze. "Ah— there's breakfast on the cart, and once you're ready we should check out and head to the airport."

He looked like he wanted to bolt. "Sean, I know I—"

"Coffee?" he asked and got to his feet, cutting off her words.

So he didn't want to talk about it. Maybe he was right. Perhaps now wasn't the time. "That would be great."

As much as she didn't want to admit it, the air between them was thick with tension and there could be only one reason why. He was clearly uncomfortable. Once they'd eaten, she showered swiftly and dressed, and was packed within the hour. Once they checked out, they took a limo to the airport and caught their flight. They were back in Rapid City by the afternoon, and he pulled up outside her father's house about forty minutes later. They had barely exchanged more than a few dozen words in the past few hours.

She turned in the seat and spoke. "Thank you… for everything. For the fun we had last night, for the lovely food and dinner, and for getting me to dress up and enjoy myself. But mostly," she said and touched his shaven jaw, "thank you for making me believe in myself. And for the opportunity. I can't tell you how much it means to me."

He nodded. "No problem. I'll talk to you soon."

He got out and extracted her bag from the back, handing it to her. He didn't walk her to the door, didn't kiss her goodbye; in fact, he didn't even wait until she was inside before he drove off. She was halfway down the hallway when she heard her father's voice and quickly joined him in the living room.

"How did it go?" Ivan asked, looking at her over the book he was reading.

She nodded and quickly explained about the contract with Vance Beaumont's hotel. "It's a big undertaking, as the space is huge and the piece will need to be big. But I can't wait to get into it."

"Looks like things are falling into place for you."

She shrugged slightly. "I hope so."

"And Sean?"

"I think…" Her words trailed off and she sighed. "I think it may have run its course."

Leah didn't need it spelled out for him. She'd told Sean she loved him, and he closed off like the proverbial clam. It was obviously over. And she was perfectly fine with that.

Positively fine.

Better than fine.

She was happy. They were over and done with, and now she could get on with what was really important. Her career. She'd had her heart broken before and she pulled through. This wouldn't be any different.

But she knew, deep down, in that place that she never let anyone see, that it *was* different. As different as night and day.

"For someone who said he wanted some company and a drink," Will said and shook his head, "you're a big disappointment. You've hardly touched that beer."

Sean stared at the bottle of amber liquid sitting in front of him. Despite insisting he wanted to get out from under the weight of his own company, he really wasn't in the mood to drink. Or socialize. He was simply tired of being alone. His friend had stopped by the house after he sent a text asking if he wanted to catch up and Sean was initially glad for the company. But now, not so much. And he refused to admit that his mood had anything to do with Leah.

Or her unexpected declaration.

I love you...

It had shocked the hell out of him.

So much so he didn't know what to do with it. What to think. And worse, what to say to her. He wasn't generally lost for words or unable to articulate his thoughts. But she'd thrown him. He wasn't ready for it. Wasn't prepared. Didn't know what to do with the sudden urge he'd had to say it back. Because it muddled his thoughts. And it polarized him. Making him vulnerable. Weak.

"I screwed up."

Will didn't look surprised. "What did you do? Get her pregnant?"

Jesus, he hoped not. "No," he said quickly. "Nothing like that. But she's…you know, invested."

"And you're not?"

Will was a good and trusted friend, but he wasn't in the mood to spill his guts and talk about his feelings for Leah.

"I don't really know."

"Well, how about we head into town for a while," Will remarked. "Play a round of pool at Rusty's?"

Sean shook his head. "No, thanks."

His friend laughed. "Man, this girl has really screwed with your brain, hasn't she? I've never seen you like this."

Because I've never been like this.

After Will left, Sean spent most of the night staring at the ceiling, missing Leah more than he would dare admit.

He hadn't seen her for four days. He'd texted a couple of times, keeping the tone light and always about her upcoming show, and her replies were the same. He'd received several RSVPs for the showing and anticipated that it would be a successful event. He knew he needed to see her though, to work through the inventory of her pieces and plan the placement at the gallery.

He rolled up at her studio at two o'clock Sunday afternoon. She wore bright orange overalls, heavy work boots and a plaid shirt, and protective glasses shielded her eyes. Sean watched her for a while, appreciating how she worked, choosing materials, creating dimensions, stepping back and then moving around the piece, her hands smoothing out the metal, her skill seducing the shape into a life of its own.

She must have sensed his intrusion, because she put down the mallet in her hand and turned, flipping up her glasses. "Oh, hi."

He walked through the doorway and moved toward her. Her hair was in a ponytail, her face free of makeup, and he thought she'd never looked more beautiful, more vibrant, more quintessentially *Leah* than she did in that moment.

"I thought we should catch up about the showing," he said easily, watching her expression narrow. "I suggest the pieces get set up on Friday."

"Actually," she said, "I've been thinking that maybe it's not such a good idea."

Sean rocked back on his heels. "You want to cancel?"

She shrugged. "I don't want to risk people not turning up like last time."

"Last time it was badly managed," he said tightly. "This time, it isn't."

"But I'm not the kind of person who likes to be in the spotlight, and I'm not good at—"

"Is this about Vegas?" he interrupted bluntly. "About what happened?"

He watched the color drain from her face. "I don't want to talk about—"

"I'm sorry, okay," he said quickly. "I'm sorry I've acted like a jerk since then. But I wasn't expecting it and didn't know how to react, and frankly, I didn't want to make things worse."

She sucked in a sharp breath. "I'm pretty sure things can't get any worse."

"You know I care about you, Leah."

She gave an annoyed groan. "Oh, please, spare me. Or better yet, forget I said what I said. In fact, forget everything about that night. Forget the past few weeks. It's what I'm trying to do. Get back to ignoring me like you've done for the past four days."

Sean propped his hands on his hips. "I wasn't ignoring you. I was giving you some space. You're angry, I get that, but I don't quite know how to handle this."

"You don't," she retorted, eyes blazing, "because I don't need to be *handled*. Forget I ever said it."

"I can't," he said. "It's out there."

"Wow, it's out there, how about we call the love police," she mocked, glaring at him. "Get over yourself, Sean, because believe me, *I* have."

It was a pointed remark, but he *didn't* believe her. Leah was a passionate, deep-feeling woman. And that made him feel like the biggest heel of all time, because she deserved way more than the meager attention he offered.

"I'm sorry that I'm not wired that way, Leah."

"How about you do us both a favor and stop talking," she insisted. "I've heard enough."

Sean's irritation grew and he turned, striding toward the door. When he reached the entrance, he stopped and exhaled heavily. He quickly swiveled around. "Okay, we'll park this conversation for the moment, but it's no reason to cancel the show at the gallery. I already have RSVPs coming back, and I'd prefer not to have to backpedal and can the whole thing. Think about your career, Leah. This is what you want, right?" he said and waved a hand in an arc at the studio. "This place, this life…so however you need to do it, muster the courage."

She was still glaring, still regarding him as though he was her least favorite person on the planet. But then she nodded. "You're right. I made a commitment to see this through, and I will. I'll borrow my brother's horse trailer to shift the bigger pieces on Friday afternoon, and the rest can go in my truck."

"Tell me what time, and I'll make sure I'm here to give you a hand."

"It's okay," she said. "Joss and Grant said they would drop by and help me take it over."

She didn't want his help. Right.

"Leah, can we just—"

"I've spoken to your mom, and the catering is all sorted and the space at the gallery will be available from Thursday," she said, cutting him off with a wave of her hand. "So everything is taken care of. I'll see you Saturday."

Sean was about to bail when he spotted a car coming up the driveway. His mom's car. Soon after his mother and Ivan got out of the vehicle.

"Book club lunch," Leah said, clearly picking up on his surprised expression. She strode through the studio and stood at the entrance, then turned back to face him. "I think our parents are dating. But I also think it's meant to be a secret. Don't ruin it for them, okay?"

Sean scowled. "You think I would?"

"What? You? The Grinch-Who-Stole-Happily-Ever-After? Of course not."

Sean's chest tightened. "Just because I didn't say that I—"

She strode off toward the car and said something to his mother. Gwen replied and looked in Sean's direction. She said something he didn't catch, and Leah quickly responded. He was grateful for the intervention as he walked toward them and stood beside Leah.

"Don't give him too hard a time," Leah said and smiled, although Sean was sure it didn't quite meet her eyes. "He's been busy planning the show at the gallery. She grabbed his arm, squeezing hard. "Oh, and considering Liam's job offer at the hotel, right?"

His mother's face creased into a broad and delighted smile. "Oh, that's wonderful. You'd be such an asset there, and I know Liam wants to step back a bit. He needs help now that Connie is about to go on maternity leave."

Sean knew that Leah knew he had no intention of accepting his brother's offer. She was simply sticking it to him because she could, and clearly got some perverse pleasure out of seeing him squirm.

"We'll see," he said and discreetly shook off her hand, even though deep down he was hungry for her touch.

"And you should tell your mom how you've said you'll donate half of your salary to the hospital," Leah said, clearly enjoying herself. "Such a generous gesture."

"Darling," his mother said and hugged him, "you really do make me proud to be your mom."

Sean forced back his scowl. "Ah, yeah, right."

He glanced toward Ivan and noticed the older man was watching the exchange with interest and wondered how much he knew about his relationship with his daughter. Not that he and Leah had a relationship. But enough, by the look on his face. He'd avoided Ivan for weeks, abandoning their chess games, and faced with it, felt like a complete coward.

"Ivan," he said as lightly as he could, "is the chessboard set up?"

The older man nodded. "Where we left it, son."

Guilt pressed down on his shoulders. "Feel like finishing that last game we started?"

Ivan grinned. "Great idea. Ladies," he said and gently slapped Sean on the shoulder. "Excuse us."

They were sitting on the veranda within minutes and Ivan made his first move. Sean tried to concentrate, tried to think about something other than the fact that Leah was alone with his mom in the studio and who knew what the hell they were discussing. Him probably.

Another ten minutes passed and they hadn't returned to the house, and figuring they were having a deep and meaningful conversation, his gut began to twitch.

"Something wrong?"

He barely registered Ivan's voice and jerked his gaze back to the game. "Ah...no."

"You know, it would be remiss of me if I didn't say that I was concerned about my daughter. But I think you know that already."

"I never meant to mislead her."

Ivan offered a quizzical look. "Is that what you've done?"

"Like I said, I didn't mean to—"

"I don't know a whole lot about women," Ivan said and grinned. "But I know they view relationships different to how we do. Take your mother, for instance. She's reluctant to get too involved because she's been hurt so badly in the past."

Sean squirmed a bit in his chair. "Ivan, I'm not sure I want to have the conversation about my mom."

"No more than I want to have it about my daughter," Ivan remarked. "But since she often comes home at eight in the morning after spending the night at your house, I have to be, well...modern in my thinking. When you have a daughter of your own, you'll understand. Leah is very emotional, which probably explains why she's so creative." Ivan sighed. "She fell fast and hard for those two idiots in her past, but I've never seen her quite like I've seen her these past weeks."

"Like what?"

Ivan sighed. "Happy. Except for these past few days. Right now, I just want to hold my little girl and make all her hurt go away. Or at least find someone who can."

Sean's chest tightened. He knew what Ivan was asking. But it was impossible.

I don't believe in love.

It doesn't last.

It ends up tasting like betrayal.

Like his parents' marriage. Like any one of the dozens of phony relationships he had witnessed over the past decade. It was better to stay away from it. Less risk.

And yet as he watched Leah and his mother walk from the studio, arms linked, he realized he was looking at the two people he loved most in the world.

And it terrified him.

Chapter Twelve

Leah couldn't stop her palms from sweating. She'd spent the better part of ninety minutes searching for something to wear to her art showing, tossing aside pantsuits, a skirt and a sensible blouse, her little black dress. None of it was truly her. In the end she settled on an ankle-length flowing multicolored skirt in soft silk, a bright orange silk halter top and a long purple coat. She teamed it with her favorite boots and big hoop earrings. The ensemble made her feel comfortable, confident and able to handle anything.

Except Sean.

She'd steered clear of him for the better part of the week, only dealing with him on a superficial level, trying to ignore that she was broken inside. He hadn't tried to talk again. He had kept his distance, just as she had told him to do. When she arrived at the gallery, Gwen, resplendent in a stylish gray pantsuit, greeted her excitedly, and Leah was delighted to see that her father had accompanied the older woman. Mitch and Tess were there, as were Winona, Grant, Hank and Joss. David and Annie, back from their honeymoon, arrived just as she was heading into the main gallery, and she hugged them both.

"This looks amazing," Annie said. "We're so proud of you."

"Thank you. I can't believe it's happening."

David hugged her. "You deserve this, sweetheart. You're so talented, and it's time the world got to see that, too."

People were starting to file into the building, more than she had expected or hoped for. The O'Sullivan clan, of course, and her own family. En masse, the Culhanes were a formidable force, and she was so glad they had all turned out to support her. Several local business owners also arrived, and she watched keenly as people continued to enter through the main doors. There was a discreet quartet in one corner, playing something classic and melodic. Waiters had begun circling the room, offering beverages and tasteful canapés. Leah politely declined a glass of wine, too nervous to drink. And she had to admit, the room, the ambience, the way her artwork was displayed on pillars or diases, showcasing each item as though it was a priceless commodity, was incredibly effective. Each piece looked impressive, important and valuable—and exactly what she had dreamed it could be.

Sean certainly knew how to pull a shindig together.

Ellie quickly found her and she hugged her cousin. "Wow, this is incredible. So where is your manager slash agent slash boyfriend?"

Leah made a face. "He's none of those things. And honestly, I don't know where he is. I thought he'd be here by now. Maybe he decided to give it a miss."

"Isn't all this his handiwork?"

She nodded. "Yes."

"I'm betting he won't miss a second."

And then she saw Sean, making his way through the crowd, slicing through people with a greeting or a nod, dressed in a dark suit that she suspected cost more than all the money she had in her checking account. He sought her out with his gaze, and her back straightened.

"Showtime," Ellie said and grinned.

Leah took a breath and walked toward him, taking the hand he held out as she approached.

"You look stunning," he said as their fingers touched. "As always."

"I'm scared out of my wits," she admitted.

"I know," he countered. "But don't be. You look incredible. Your work is outstanding. And you're with me. You got this."

You're with me...

It sounded so natural. So…real. But it wasn't true. She wasn't with him. She offered her love and he'd shut down. This was business for him. She was his pet pity project. Something to keep his mind occupied.

"There are so many people here," she proclaimed. "I have no idea how you pulled this off."

"I know people."

"Do you mean you say jump and people say how high?"

He chuckled. "Not exactly. But I called in a few favors."

"For me?"

"For you," he replied.

She looked across the room and spotted a tall man in an outrageously flamboyant orange and white suit. "Isn't that…" Her words trailed as she tried to recall a name. "Isn't he famous? Some sort of musician?"

Sean smiled and led her toward the man. "Rapper. And yes, he's very famous. I'll introduce you. He has a mansion in Beverly Hills that really could do with one of your sculptures in the foyer."

The following hours felt like a dream, and not the nightmare she'd always imagined. Instead of hiding from the attention, she embraced it. Instead of thinking her work wasn't good enough…that *she* wasn't good enough, Leah experienced an overwhelming sense of empowerment. And somehow, her doubts and resistance disappeared. She talked to people she'd never dared to imagine she would talk to. She discussed her art with prospective buyers. She referenced her sources of inspiration—from the Black Hills to the local indigenous people, to the colors of the sky and trees to the beauty of the river itself. And people listened. No one mocked her or thought she was weird. No one judged her. She was an artist showcasing her art. She was exactly who she wanted to be. And amazingly, she sold her work—several pieces in fact—and took orders for half a dozen more.

When it was over, when the last of the invited guests left and she was alone with Sean, Ellie, David and Annie and Gwen and her father, Leah slid into a chair, completely exhausted. But also elated. Not in her wildest dreams had she believed anything so wonderful could happen to her.

Everyone was talking among themselves, discussing the evening. Except for Sean. He stood off to one side, near the largest of her sculptures, which had found a home with the rap star. She got to her feet and walked over, standing beside him, close enough that she knew only he would hear her every word.

"How did you really do it?" she asked. "How did you get so many celebrities and successful business people to come to a small town in South Dakota, to see an art exhibit for an unknown, insignificant artist?"

He looked at her. "Ten years of experience in how to handle people."

"Like Vance Beaumont?" she asked. "Who owed you a favor?"

He nodded. "Well, yeah. And like the rapper came to my studio six years ago with good lyrics, lots of heart and no money. I gave him a chance to realize his dream and he hasn't forgotten that. The world is full of talented, creative people like yourself, Leah... sometimes all you need is one person to believe in you and the rest takes care of itself."

He was right. And he was also that one person who believed in her. Whatever had transpired between them, she could never repay him for his support and encouragement. No one had ever believed in her so much.

"Thank you," she said shakily. "For everything you've done. For helping me believe in myself. I'm not sure how I can ever repay you."

"I don't want or need repayment."

Leah shuddered back a breath. "Can I ask you something? *Why* did you do all this? What's in it for you?"

"Seeing you shine," he replied. "Like you did tonight. You're glowing, Leah. You're doing what you were meant to do, what you were *made* to do. That's payment enough."

"But the hotel in Vegas, the airplane tickets, the limos, the way you arranged all this so effortlessly... I need to settle the tab."

"I thought of something...you could stop hating me."

She swallowed hard. "I don't hate you."

"You don't?"

Leah shook her head. "No, I don't. The truth is, I love you."

His gaze narrowed. "That might just gratitude talking."

"It's not," she admitted. "It's my heart talking. I know you're not in love with me, Sean. I also know I promised that this wouldn't happen...that we'd keep it casual. I know I'm not even your type. But I can't help how I feel...just as you can't help how you feel."

She stood on her toes and kissed his cheek, inhaling the woodsy masculine scent that was uniquely his. He didn't flinch. And she knew it was over. They were done.

"I'll drive you home."

She shook her head. "No, I'll drive myself." She smiled at him. "Thank you for being you."

And that, she thought, was the end of it.

Sean was back in Rapid City the following Tuesday for his follow-up hearing appointment. He went through the same discussion with the audiologist, and for the first time, talked about the possibility of hearing aids. It was a hard conversation—one of the hardest of his life. But he listened and took the reading material he was given. He had a lot to think about. A lot to consider.

Once he left the appointment Sean texted his mother and said he wanted to catch up with her the following day, knowing he couldn't avoid it any longer.

He thought about hanging around town for a while, maybe grabbing lunch, but he was tired of his own company. He'd parked across the street and pulled his keys from his pocket. It was windy day, miserable by the usual standards, but the streets were busy since it was less than a couple of weeks to go until Christmas. The holidays were coming up. He knew what to expect. Family and presents and suffocating concern. He'd considered taking off for a few days, and then knew his mother wouldn't forgive him if he bailed. Which meant he needed to start thinking about shopping. Usually he sent gift baskets. They were easy and no fuss. This year he figured he wasn't going to get away with so little effort.

Sean looked at the department store down the block, and since he had some free time, quickly changed direction and stepped off the sidewalk. In a split second he heard a voice, like someone yelling, but it seemed far away. Only it wasn't. And within seconds there was another sound, this one screeching, and suddenly a bicycle collided directly with his left side and sent him flying across the pavement. He experienced a sharp and searing pain as he hit the ground, and had the fleeting thought that he hoped there was no other traffic coming as the last thing he wanted was to be hit by a bus. He also wondered if he was going to hit his head and black out. Or worse.

It took about two seconds for mayhem to ensue

and ten minutes for an ambulance to arrive. He was quickly attended by the paramedics and transported to the local hospital.

An hour and half later he was diagnosed with a broken left arm, which wasn't surprising because it had twisted to a weird angle and hurt like hell. All he wanted to do was to get the damned thing set in a cast and get out of the ER's triage area. But no such luck. For one, he couldn't drive. And the cyclist was in the next bed, dealing with a multitude of scratches and abrasions, but thankfully nothing worse. Out of options, Sean grabbed his cell and looked through his stored numbers, finding the one he wanted.

It was answered on the third ring.

"I need your help," he said and briefly explained what had happened. "And don't tell anyone else, okay?"

Twenty minutes later his half brother walked into triage.

"Thanks for coming," Sean said flatly.

Jonah was frowning, an expression he was familiar with, since he wore it well himself. "No problem. Happy to help."

Sean had called him because he worked in Rapid City at an architectural firm and was close at hand.

"How did it happen?" Jonah asked.

He explained about the accident and jerked a thumb in the direction of the cyclist, shrugging. "Just one of those things."

The teenager in the neighboring hospital bed

glanced over. "I'm sorry, man, this has never happened to me before. My grandma is gonna kill me when she finds out I wrecked my bike."

Sean managed to nod, despite the fact he was now aching all over. "I'll replace your bike. Don't stress."

The teen looked relieved. "Thanks, man. I need my wheels to get to school. I kept ringing my bell and yelling, and I couldn't stop because there was a car behind me."

He looked at the distraught teenager, and seconds later a harried looking older woman in a waitress uniform came bursting into triage and quickly headed for the teenager. "Mikey, are you okay? Are you badly hurt?"

It took only a moment to work out the dynamic between them—a parentless teen, a loving and clearly overworked grandparent. And Sean's guilt quickly trebled. He was a stubborn fool.

"I'm sorry, kid," he said and then looked at his brother. "I want to tell you something."

Jonah sat on the chair next to the bed and listened as Sean quickly explained about his hearing loss. Unlike Kieran, Jonah didn't shoot out a bunch of questions—just one.

"How come you haven't told Dad and Gwen?"

Sean sucked in a breath. "Because you know what they're like. They'll…"

"Smother you with love and concern?" his brother suggested.

"Yeah," he replied, his stomach sinking when he realized how idiotic that actually sounded.

"I get it," Jonah replied. "But if you don't want it, don't accept it. Just tell them and then move on as though nothing has changed."

"Except things have changed," Sean reminded him. "I sold my business, left my life behind, came back to a town I've never felt like I truly belonged to."

"Then why did you?" Jonah asked the obvious question and didn't wait for a reply. "Because you wanted connection? Family? I get that, too. Have you ever thought that maybe this is where you were meant to be all along? Granted, this isn't how anyone imagined your homecoming."

He knew what his brother meant. "Are you saying it's fate?"

Jonah nodded. "Well, if Liam and Kayla hadn't eloped and you guys had never found out about me, then I'd probably still be stuck in Portland, still hating J.D. and resenting the family I had never known. I'd never have met Connie, wouldn't have a baby on the way, wouldn't be right here, talking to you. So, I think that sometimes fate gives us exactly what we need, right when we need it. Maybe just not the way we would expect." He smiled. "Maybe you're thinking too hard. It's what we do."

The more Sean considered it, the more alike they seemed. "What if you couldn't be an architect anymore? What would you do?"

"I'd find something else I was good at," Jonah replied. "Like, maybe running a hotel."

"Liam told you about that?"

Jonah nodded. "It's not a bad idea. Although I bet you could stay in the music industry, too, if you really wanted, too. If that art exhibition is anything to go by, you seem pretty good at handling people and managing and promoting events. You know, saying the right things, working a room, so to speak. You seem to have a knack for being charming," Jonah added and grinned. "Well, to most people."

Sean sighed heavily. "I've spent the last couple of years really wanting to hate you."

"I know," Jonah said.

"I guess I blamed you for my folks breaking up."

"I know that, too," his brother remarked. "Don't feel alone. I've done my share of blaming in the past."

"How'd you get through it?"

"Connie," Jonah replied simply, and his expression softened. "She made me see the world differently. She got me to see past the anger and resentment. I guess she helped me become a better man."

Sean's chest tightened. He didn't want to think about it. Didn't want to imagine that he'd been close to finding that same sense of peace. "How did she do that?"

Jonah shrugged. "She loved me. Although I never quite understood why. Sometimes I still don't. But she makes me want to be the best version of myself. She also made me realize I had to embrace forgiveness. I had to forgive Dad," he said and sighed heavily. "For lying and deceiving everyone. But mostly, I had to forgive myself for being the cause of all the chaos."

His brother's words struck a chord deep down. Forgiveness? Had he ever truly experienced that? Had he ever opened himself up to something so raw?

"I hate the lies Dad told."

"Me too," Jonah said.

"It's like he made a mockery of the happy family I thought we had. And I think I blamed Liz for dying," he admitted out loud for the first time in his life, his throat burning.

"Understandable," Jonah remarked. "You guys were close."

"When we were kids, Liam and Kieran were always this tight unit, you know, like they were best friends as well as brothers. I think Liz knew I always felt left out and tried to make me a part of things. My mom was great, always there, always available... but Dad was... I don't know, emotionally absent."

Jonah nodded slowly. "For me he was physically absent. I guess we both got the thing he could easily give."

For the first time, Sean understood. While J.D. had been living in Cedar River and raising his family, his heart had been in Portland, with the woman he loved and the son he couldn't really claim. It made him think about Leah, too. About how she'd opened herself up to him and he'd shut her down with his silence.

"I need a favor," Sean said.

"Name it."

"I can't drive with a broken arm. Once I'm out of here, I need you to drive me back to the audiologist," he said and met his brother's gaze. "And then I'd appreciate it if you could take me to see our father."

"What are you going to do?" Jonah asked, looking a little wary.

Sean sucked in a breath. "I'm going to face the enemy."

"You mean J.D.?"

"No," he replied. "I mean me. I mean my ego, and my pride."

Decorating the Christmas tree within an inch of its life at the Triple C ranch with the other women in the family was a family tradition, and Leah always enjoyed the occasion and the event had become quite the bonding session. There was also wine. Not too much, because Tess was still nursing Charlie and Abby had announced she was pregnant.

There was, she thought, a whole lot of hormones in the room. And happiness. She longed to feel a connection, to be a part of things, to forge her own sense of belonging with the women she cared about most. But in that moment, she simply felt alone and excluded.

Christmas was just over a week away, and she

should have been jumping out of her skin with happiness because life was so amazing. She had money in the bank. Several pieces of her art had already been shipped off, and she had enough work ordered to be busy for the next six months. She had even bought a new truck, since her old one was on the way out and she needed a reliable vehicle to haul materials for her work. Yes, she should have been ecstatic.

But she wasn't happy. She was miserable. And she'd been hibernating like a bear, hanging out in her studio until late at night, not talking, avoiding her father, and particularly avoiding Gwen when she stopped by. The last thing she wanted to do was have a heart-to-heart with Sean's mother.

"So, Winona and I were thinking you should have a big birthday bash," Ellie announced and looked at Leah as she climbed down the ladder after placing the star on top of the huge tree. "It's not every day that a girl turns twenty-eight."

The other woman all chuckled. But Leah wasn't smiling. Because her birthday coincided with Valentine's Day, which would quickly loom once the holidays were over, and she had no real interest in celebrating either event in her current state of mind.

"I'll think about it," she replied in her usual friendly way, and then decided that she wasn't going to be swayed and suddenly stood her ground. "Actually, no, I'd prefer to keep it on the down low. You all know I hate being the center of attention."

Ellie grinned. "You managed to handle the pressure at the gallery show last week."

"That was different," she remarked. "That was work."

And because she had someone at her side the entire evening. Someone who had her back and protected her from the hard questions, from ridicule, from failure. Something she was certain the other women all knew, but were too polite to say anything because she'd made a point of not mentioning Sean for days. To anyone.

"How is Sean, by the way?" Abby asked. "Recovering well?"

Leah's gaze narrowed. "What do you mean?"

"After the accident yesterday," she replied.

Leah's breath stilled in her lungs. Abby was the head chef at the O'Sullivan Hotel and was privy to the goings-on with the family.

Not like me.

"I don't know anything about…" Her words trailed off, and she could see the sympathy in the other woman's eyes. In everyone's eyes.

"He's out of the hospital," Abby said quickly. "It was just an ER visit. All I know is that he was hit by a car or a bike or something and is—"

White noise screeched so loud in her brain, Leah thought she might pass out. She jumped to her feet, her hands shaking. "I have to go."

Leah grabbed her tote and raced out of the ranch house, ignoring Mitch and Jake as she passed them in the hallway. She tried Sean's cell the moment she got into her truck, and it went directly to voice mail. Frantic, she considered calling Gwen, but her pride got firmly stuck in her throat. He hadn't called her. *No one* had called her. It was as though she wasn't on his radar, or the radar of anyone associated with him.

She drove to his house in record time, but he wasn't home. She tried calling his cell again, but no luck, and then headed into town, gravitating to the hotel. Liam would know, she thought. Liam wouldn't care that she was asking after his brother. Unlike Gwen, who would see the pathetic love in her eyes. She raced to the concierge and asked to speak to Liam. Of course the girl behind the desk knew who she was. Her art piece was conspicuous in the foyer, and she had been to the hotel many times.

Minutes later Liam appeared, in his corporate jacket and tie.

"Leah, are you okay?" he asked, clearly taking in her harried expression and looking worried. "My mom and dad are here if you need—"

"Where is he?" she asked quickly.

One dark brow rose. "Ah… I guess you mean Sean? He's upstairs."

My God, was he so badly injured he needed a room at the hotel instead of his own house? Did he need looking after? Was he bedridden? Why hadn't someone called her? She was so overwrought she wanted to scream. "Can I see him?"

Liam's mouth hitched at one side for a second,

and then he nodded. "Sure," he said and ushered her toward the elevator. He used his pass card to open the door and pressed a couple of buttons once she was inside. "Third floor, second door on the right."

He stepped out and the doors closed, and within seconds she was headed upward. When the doors swooshed open, she hurried out and realized she was in the corporate suite, not a level with guest rooms.

Leah walked down the hall, passing one door, then stopping outside the second door on the right. It was open and led to a moderate size office. There was a desk a little way from the doorway, a couple of narrow couches and then another doorway, also open. She walked inside, noticing the flowers on the desk, the subtle scent of a woman's fragrance in the air. She had the illogical thought that he was with someone and then decided she shouldn't care. They'd made no promise to one another. He'd made it clear he didn't want her to care about him.

Then why am I here?

Because she did care. She loved him. And the very idea that he was hurt and she didn't know made her ache down deep in her bones. Leah took a breath and walked toward the open door, halting on the threshold. Sean was by the window, wearing jeans and a T-shirt, his leather jacket slung over the big desk that was in the center of the room.

And his left arm was in a cast.

He turned, as though sensing her presence, and Leah almost crumpled to the ground. He had a graze on his forehead and another on his chin. She fought the urge to rush over and hold him in her arms. He didn't want her arms. He didn't want her anything.

"Leah," he said her name on a sigh. "Hey there."

She remained where she was. "So it's true about the accident? You're hurt?"

He glanced at his arm and shrugged with the other shoulder. "I'm okay. Nothing life-threatening."

"I called you earlier," she said. "It went to voice mail."

He nodded. "I accidently left my cell at the hospital in Rapid City yesterday. I need to go and get it at some point, but driving is out right now. I broke my arm," he said, stating the obvious.

Leah took a step forward, sucking in some air, so mad she could barely speak. But she did.

"And you didn't have the decency to let me know?"

"I was going to—"

"Are you that insensitive that you couldn't spare two minutes to let me know you'd been hit by a car?" she said, cutting him off, her hands waving angrily.

He actually had the audacity to look shocked by her tone. "Ah…bike," he corrected and then dared to half smile. "I stepped off the sidewalk and was hit by a kid on a bicycle."

"I don't care if it was a Mack truck," she said heatedly. "You *should* have told me."

She sucked in a sharp breath and took a couple steps closer, really looking at him. And then she noticed the difference in his demeanor and quickly understood.

"You're…you're…"

He nodded. "Yes, I am wearing hearing aids," he said and motioned to the small devices behind his ears.

Leah was surprised. "You kept saying you weren't ready."

He looked a little sheepish, and her heart tightened. "I thought I wasn't. But being knocked on my ass yesterday because I didn't hear the bicycle coming changed things. The truth is, *I've* changed."

"I guess you have," she said.

He stepped forward. "Leah, I've been trying to—"

"Forget me?" she challenged, angry and hurt and disregarded, and feeling all the things she felt at the hands of Gary Billings and Xavier. Only this was much worse. Because this was Sean, and she loved him to the very depths of her soul and he didn't return those feelings. "Trying to erase me from your memory as though it never happened because I'm so not in your league and am so easily forgettable."

More shock, this time countered by a spark of annoyance in his eyes. "Of course not. If you'll let me explain, we can—"

"Explain what, Sean?" she demanded. "I've been this foolish girl before, remember?"

"What does that mean?"

She gave a brittle laugh. "Oh, you know, in over my head? Falling for the wrong man? Well, guess what," she said, strength returning to her limbs, her blood, her very soul. "I'm actually *not* that girl anymore, the one who didn't have enough value on herself and let people walk all over her. I guess I should thank you for helping me overcome my polarizing insecurity. Because, guess what, I'm strong and confident and way too smart to waste any more time pining over a guy like you!"

She turned on her heel and left the room, almost bumping directly into Liam, J.D. and Gwen on her way out, feeling exhilarated, feeling strength seep into her bones with every step.

And feeling like *herself* for the first time in her life.

Chapter Thirteen

Sean slumped back into the chair and held the cast on his arm close to his chest. He'd never seen Leah so angry. So compelling. And utterly lovely, despite the rage clearly coursing through her veins.

He looked up and spotted Liam and their parents standing in the doorway.

"I guess you heard that?" Sean asked.

Liam shrugged. "Enough. She must be crazy in love with you to yell at you like that."

He tried to smile and failed. "I'm pretty sure she hates me right now."

"She'll get over it," Liam remarked. "The only woman who ever got *that* mad with me is Kayla. And look at us now."

Sean still couldn't smile. Because he didn't like seeing Leah upset—particularly when he knew he was the cause.

"Maybe I should go after her?" his mother suggested.

Sean didn't respond, because he wasn't sure what Leah needed in that moment. Perhaps comfort from a mother figure was *exactly* what she needed to ease the hurt in her heart. A hurt he knew he was responsible for.

"Mom, Dad," Sean said, not bothering to hide his skepticism. "Did you guys ever really love each other?"

"Of course," J.D. replied quickly.

His mother regarded him thoughtfully. "I know your dad's married to Kathleen now, but that doesn't make our marriage any less real. I'll always be grateful for what we had and for the four amazing children we had. There were a lot of good years together."

Sean listened to his mother's words, trying to find solace. And somehow, amid all the chaos screaming in his head, he did. So maybe his parents didn't have a perfect relationship or one that went the distance, but his mother was right—it didn't mean it wasn't real and valuable.

He took a deep breath. "I need to talk to you," he said and moved closer to them. "I know you've all been wondering why I sold my business and came back to Cedar River. The truth is, a year ago I was diagnosed with something called sensorineural hearing loss. I'm slowly losing my hearing—now it's to the point that I need to wear aids," he said and gestured to the devices behind his ears.

Sean met his mother's gaze, saw her concerned expression quickly turn into something he didn't expect—relief.

"Oh, Sean," she said and promptly hugged him. "I've been so worried—I know it must be terrible for you, but I'm so relieved you've finally told us. I really have been imagining the worst."

"Mom, I—"

"Why didn't you tell us sooner?" his father asked, cutting him off.

Sean shook his head. "Oh, you know, my pride got in the way. I'm sorry. I should have come to you, but I just wasn't ready to talk about it."

They talked for a few minutes about his diagnosis and the next steps he planned to take—the lessons he'd arranged in ASL in Rapid City, his next appointment with the specialist—and he noticed how caringly his parents accepted his explanation. Which of course they would, he realized. If he'd ever doubted how much his family cared, those doubts quickly disappeared.

"By the way, Kieran and Jonah already know, so don't be mad at them for not saying anything. I swore them to secrecy so I could tell you myself." He turned to face his father. "And I've made peace with Jonah. I know he's not to blame for you and

Mom splitting up. He's my brother," he said. "Actually, he's all right. I even kind of like him."

J.D. grinned broadly. "Thank you, son. That means a lot."

Sean glanced at Liam. "Oh, and I'll come and work at the hotel for a while," he said and saw his brother's startled look. "I'll help out while Connie's on maternity leave."

Liam's brows came up. "And after that?"

"We'll see. I've got a few ideas. And I'll probably want to change some things around here," Sean said and grinned. "You know me."

"I'm hoping so," Liam replied. "You bring a whole different perspective to the table, and I'm looking forward to any changes for the better. But honestly, after nearly ten years of running this place, I'm ready to step back a bit. The hospital has offered me a position on the board. I think they're hoping I can help solicit donations for the new surgical wing."

"I'm sure you'll be doing your fair share of donating, too," Sean corrected.

His brother smiled. "It's easier to give when you have a lot. And frankly, I feel as though I have everything a man could want. A great job, a beautiful wife and kids, a lovely home."

Sean met his gaze. "What does that feel like? Having…everything?"

"Why don't you find out for yourself?"

A tremor shook him. Because for the first time in

his life, he could admit that he did want it. Like he wanted air to breath and the ground beneath his feet.

"By the way, I want half my salary given to the hospital."

Liam looked at him. "What? Why?"

He sighed. "A promise I made to a friend. And to Mom."

"A friend?"

"Leah," he admitted. "I'm in love with her."

Neither his parents or brother looked surprised by his declaration and it made him smile. For weeks he'd been in a cocoon of denial, refusing to admit the obvious—that after so many years of being away, he had finally come home. And with that, he'd been forced to face the truth about who and what he was.

Scared. Angry. Resentful.

Scared to let anyone see that he'd given up his career—that because of his failing hearing, he felt unable to control his own destiny for the first time in his life. And then he was angry at the world, but mostly at himself for being so weak. And resentful of the family—particularly Jonah and his father, with whom he had felt so estranged. But the estrangement was of his own doing.

And while all that was going on…something else happened.

He met Leah.

Someone who saw him—flaws and all. And for reasons he only now understood, someone he allowed to see those flaws. And she didn't run. She witnessed him being hurt and angry and didn't bail. Instead, she became his friend. And then his lover. And then, without asking anything in return, the love of his life.

And he'd hurt her, saying nothing, refusing to admit what was in his heart because he was afraid it wouldn't last. That he would be left. Deceived. Humiliated. Like his father had humiliated his mother, and by association, the whole family. She'd admitted what she was feeling, and he should have embraced it, honored it. And more importantly, said it back.

Because he loved her, wholly and completely, and wanted both Leah and the world to know it. He wanted to run down Main Street, shouting it at the top of his lungs…anything and everything so she would know she was all he wanted and needed.

She was angry with him, that was for sure, but what they had between them was worth fighting for, even if it meant complete and total humiliation.

Sean experienced an unfamiliar and warm sort of peace flowing through his blood and suddenly knew what he needed to do. He had to make things right. He had to grovel. He had to prove that he was serious.

But mostly, he had to make her see that he was worthy of her love.

Leah drove through the gates of the Triple C Ranch on Sunday morning. She felt stronger than she had for days. Christmas was looming and she still had a few gifts to buy, and planned to head into Rapid City the following day to finish her shopping and collect some materials for the latest piece she was working on. But first she had plans to ride Chico for a while, and make arrangements to purchase him from her cousin. She was surprised to see her brother's SUV parked outside the house, but was always glad to see her only sibling.

David and Mitch were on the porch and she strode up the pathway, reminded about how only weeks ago she'd met Sean on the same spot. Back when they were friends. Back before they were lovers. And the memory was so acute, it made her ache down to her bones.

"Hey," she said as she approached, her boots clicking on the steps. Both men greeted her with a smile, and she returned the gesture. "I've come to make you an offer," she said to her cousin.

Mitch's brow rose quickly. "You have?"

Leah planted her hands on her jean-clad hips. "Well, you may have heard that I recently had quite a successful art exhibition?"

"Yes," he said and grinned. "I was there, remember?"

Leah chuckled. "Well, I actually sold a few pieces that night and have several orders that will keep me busy for a while. Plus I am doing a piece for a hotel lobby in Las Vegas."

"So, fame and fortune are knocking?" Mitch teased. "That's great news."

"Well, the fame is in the long game, but I have made a little money. So," she said and took a long breath, "I'd like to make you an offer to buy Chico."

Mitch looked at her, then glanced toward David, and after the longest moment, he shook his head. "Ah, sorry, Leah—you're too late."

Her stomach sank. "Too late? What do you mean?"

Mitch sighed. "I sold Chico yesterday. Dropped him off to his new owner this morning."

Her sinking stomach plummeted, and she could barely breathe. "I don't understand. I thought… I didn't think you were planning on selling him to anyone else, and I—"

"I had an offer I couldn't refuse."

She knew the horse was worth a lot. "How much?" He named the figure and her eyes bulged. "Oh my God. I mean, I knew he was valuable, but never in a million years would I have imagined that—"

"Leah," her brother said, cutting her off, "you need to have this conversation with your boyfriend."

Leah stilled instantly. "My what?"

"O'Sullivan dropped by yesterday," Mitch replied. "Made the offer and said whatever anyone else offered he would triple it."

Leah sucked in a sharp breath, rooted to the spot. "He did what?"

"Handed over a big wad of cash and asked me to drop Chico off at his place this morning, which I did. Nice place he's got there, by the way. He must have about seven acres or so, prime real estate on the river, too."

All Leah heard was *blah, blah, blah.* "He doesn't even like horses!"

"Really?" David questioned. "Go figure."

Leah didn't bother hiding her anger and confusion. First her house, now her horse? "Why would he do this?"

David shrugged. "Like I said, looks like you guys need to talk."

"I don't want to talk to him," she argued.

"Yeah," Mitch said and grinned. "He said that. Told us you were mad at him for being a jackass, or something like that."

"I am mad at him," she agreed. "And I'm even madder now."

"Better go and confront him then," David suggested. "And find out what he's up to."

Leah looked at her brother and cousin in turn and saw they were smiling. "What's going on?"

David shrugged innocently. "Beats me. You're the one with the billionaire boyfriend who just bought the horse you love, a horse he'll never ride, for three times its value."

"He's not a billionaire," she contradicted, not really having any idea if he was or wasn't.

"You sure about that?" David queried.

"Well, no," she replied. "Anyway, I don't care if he is or isn't." She had a thought and glared at Mitch. "And for the record, he's not my boyfriend. But if you accepted three times Chico's value, then you should be ashamed of yourself. Since when do you take advantage of people?"

"I don't," Mitch replied. "He's pretty persuasive though. For a moment I thought he was going to throw in the Ferrari. But then he said he was selling it and buying an SUV."

Leah scowled. "I have no idea what you're talking about."

"We know," David said, sounding exasperated. "So go and find out. You know you want to."

"I don't want anything to do with him," she retorted. "Particularly now that I know he's robbed me of my horse."

Both men laughed. "He was right," David said and looked toward Mitch for a moment before meeting her gaze. "O'Sullivan said you'd be too proud and angry to face him."

"He did, did he?" she asked, outraged. "Ha! He thinks he knows me so well."

She was down the steps and back in her truck without saying another word. The drive to his home was long and tense, and she barreled down his driveway faster than she would normally have done. Leah spotted Chico the moment she cleared the trees, prancing around his new paddock, clearly having a great time as he raced in and out of the stable.

Leah pulled up outside his house, got out of the truck and halted when she saw Sean sitting on the front steps, elbows on his knees, looking as though he'd been expecting her.

"You knew I was coming?" she demanded, standing ten feet away from him.

He nodded. "Your brother texted me."

Her blood boiled. "Since when are you and my brother texting buddies?"

"It's a recent development."

Leah glared long and hard. "You bought my horse?"

"I did," he replied.

"Why?"

"I needed a way to get your attention."

She had no idea why. "By taking what's mine?" she asked and waved an arm dramatically, gesturing around, being irrational and not caring because she was so hurt and angry she couldn't help herself. "Like this house. And now Chico. You really are—"

"I bought the horse for you," he said flatly, still sitting.

Leah stilled, her arms falling to her sides. "You did? Why?"

"Because you wanted him."

It wasn't nearly enough of an answer. "Being rich doesn't give you a free pass when it comes to explaining your motives. And my cousin ripped you off," she added.

"Not his fault. I threw out a number and wasn't leaving until he accepted."

Leah's annoyance spiked. "Typical O'Sullivan behavior," she muttered.

"Well, that's what I am," he said quickly. "By the way, I've told my family everything. They were really supportive. I've even made up with my dad and Jonah."

Leah didn't know what to say. What to think. He looked earnest. Regretful. *Sorry.*

But she was too raw to imagine any of it had to do with her. "I'm happy for you."

"Are you?" he asked, stepping closer. "Happy, I mean?"

No. She was so unhappy it seemed to be clinging to every cell she possessed. "Over the moon," she replied. "I start designing the Beaumont piece next week. I have money in the bank thanks to your rapper friend. My life is sweet. Perfect. Exactly as I wanted it."

"Is it?" he queried.

Heat clawed at her throat. She wasn't going to fall apart. She wasn't going to let him see *how wretchedly unhappy* she was because she'd hadn't seen him for days. Or how much she missed his smile. His frown. The feel of his arms around her. The taste of his kiss. Instead, she concentrated on the obvious. "Why did you really buy him?" she asked and hooked a thumb in the direction of the corral.

"For you," he replied. "A grand gesture."

Leah scowled. "What does that mean?"

"It means," he said and sighed, "that I knew the

horse was precious to you, and I didn't want to risk him not being yours. So, yeah, I bought him, and yeah, I'm giving him to you."

"I can't accept him," she said, dying inside.

"Why not?"

"Because that kind of grand gesture is for people who...you know...people who are together and have feelings that—"

"Leah, I screwed up," he said, cutting her off. "So badly. I've wanted to say so many things to you and haven't been able to admit to any of them." He ran a hand through his hair. "That night...that night in Las Vegas when you said what you said, I was shocked. I admit it. I didn't know how to respond, and so I backed off... I turned away from you and I know that hurt you." He stopped, his voice shaking a little, his blue eyes dragging back to hers even though he looked as though he wanted to look anywhere else but at her. "And I'm so, so sorry."

Heat burned behind her eyes and she blinked, fighting back the tears she knew threatened to spill over. "It's okay, Sean. I mean, I know you can't feel things to order and we did start out saying we would just be friends with—"

"I wasn't ready for it," he admitted, cutting her off again. "I'd *never* been ready to hear it."

"Why?" she asked, agonized and scared as she waited for his reply.

"Because I have always believed it wasn't real and that it didn't last," he stated, his voice raw with emotion. "And when you said what you said, I panicked… I thought about my parents and remembered all the lousy relationships I'd witnessed in the last decade and did the unthinkable—I hurt you." He stepped close, his blue eyes glittering, and grabbed her hand, holding it tightly within his own. "What you deserved, what I should have done when you said what you said, was to say it back." He inhaled heavily again and swallowed hard. "Because, Leah, of course I'm in love with you."

Leah's heart surged, and the tears she was fighting immediately spilled down her cheeks. "But you said you didn't believe in love."

"I know what I said," he replied, urging her closer. "I was stupid and thoughtless."

"I'm not your type," she reminded him.

"Yes, you are," he assured her, bringing her into contact with his lean length. "And I'm yours. We are imperfectly perfect for one another. I love your creativity and your beautiful smile and your amazing rainbow hair. I love how loving you makes me feel alive. Please," he said, bringing her hand to his mouth and gently kissing her knuckles. "Give me a chance. Give us a chance."

Leah had never heard more beautiful words in her life. And she wanted to believe them so much, with every part of her aching and love-starved heart. "Give you a chance?"

"To prove that I'm worthy enough," he said. "To deserve you."

Leah's insides soared. "Oh, Sean," she said and reached out to touch his face. "I think that's the most romantic thing anyone has ever said to me."

He gathered her close. "Can we go inside and get out of this cold?"

She nodded and minutes later they were in the living room, sitting together on the sofa, hands entwined. She took a long breath and spoke. "Are you sure?"

"That I love you?" He grinned. "Positive. Believe me, no one could be more shocked by this than me," he admitted and smiled ruefully. "I mean, I'm not exactly known for my ability to commit. But these last few days, imagining that I'd lost you, was killing me."

Leah sighed and leaned toward him. He kissed her hotly, moving his mouth over hers as he gently anchored her head with one hand. When the kiss ended, she was breathless.

She gestured to one hearing aid. "I'm so proud of you for taking this step."

His eyes glittered even more. "It wasn't easy, you know, admitting that I needed help. But they're small and discreet and work well."

Leah's gaze sharpened when she realized something else. "Does this mean you're going back to LA? Your career...are you planning on—"

"No," he said, gently cutting her off as he touched her cheek. "My life is in Cedar River...with you. And for the moment, so is my job," he announced and grinned and quickly explained about working at the hotel for a while. "It'll be fun and it's not forever. At some point I want to get back to working in the music industry. I'm not sure what just yet, but I'll take some time and think about what I really want to do. I might open up a studio again, who knows. I've made a lot of contacts over the years, and working on your art show was really rewarding—so perhaps I'll look at promoting instead of producing. But, whatever I do, the most important thing will be loving you, everyday, for the rest of my life."

"Oh, Sean," she said and sighed. "I love you so much. I was so worried about you when I found out you were hurt."

He rubbed her cheek with his thumb. "I'm sorry I didn't call you right away. I guess I got caught up settling things with my family, and I wanted to make sure the air was clear before I tried to make amends with you. How am I doing so far?"

She grinned. "Pretty good."

"God, you're easy on me," he said and sighed. "I'm sure I don't deserve it after the way I acted."

Leah's insides tightened and she shook her head. "You know, I haven't exactly made things easy. I have a bad temper, and I'm way too emotional and take things to heart."

"You're perfect," he contradicted. "And beautiful and talented and the best friend I have ever had."

"Gosh, you can be sweet." She sighed. "But you're right. I love that we were friends first. And I love that you saw what I needed…someone to believe in me. I feel as though I finally have the chance to be the artist that I'm meant to be. And that," she said pointedly, "is all because of you. Remember how I said there were only two men I trusted?" She shook her head. "There are three."

"Thank you," he said softly. "That means a lot."

He smiled and then kissed her, long and slow, and she kissed him back, holding his shoulders. When he pulled back, he was smiling.

"You know, this house is really too big for one. So," he said and took a breath. "When you're certain your dad will be okay living on his own—or when he and my mom finally admit how they feel about one another—what do you say about moving in here with me? The dogs can come too, since they already adore me."

Leah swallowed the lump in her throat. "I'd like that."

"We can set up another studio in the boathouse," he suggested, and then hesitated for a second. "And then, once we've spent way more time together, if it's okay with you, I intend to ask you to marry me. Because I'd really love to be your husband, Leah. And maybe, when we're ready, start a family one day."

"Kids?" she queried and smiled deeply.

He nodded. "What do you think?" he ventured. "Do you think you'd say yes?"

Leah absorbed him, seeing the love in his eyes, seeing everything she had ever wanted. And more. All her fears slipped away, along with the memory of anyone else she'd ever loved. She smiled, taking his hand and linking their fingers and saying exactly what was in her heart.

"I do."

* * * * *

*After a fight over Susannah's plans for her deceased
sister's frozen embryos strained their friendship,
Gabe comes home to Texas to find Susannah's a single
parent—of toddler quintuplets! And he wants to help.
Can he and Susannah work together for the big family
they've always desired?*

Read on for a sneak peek at
His Plan for the Quintuplets,
*the first book in Cathy Gillen Thacker's
new miniseries,* Lockharts Lost & Found.

Tears continuing to spill from her eyes, she pushed away
from him and let out a shuddering breath. Her chest rose
and fell with each agitated breath. "Just…everything."
She gestured helplessly.

"Are you worried about the kids?" Given what Mitzy
had showed her, she shouldn't be.

"No." Susannah took another halting breath, still
struggling to get her emotions under control. "You saw
them," she said, making no effort to hide her aggravation
with herself. "They were thrilled. They always are when
they get to spend time with the other dads."

"Which is something they don't have."

She pressed on the bridge of her nose. "Right." She swallowed and finally looked up at him again, remorse glimmering in her sea-blue eyes. "It just makes me feel guilty sometimes, because I know they're never going to have that."

He brought her back into the curve of his arm. "You don't know that," he said gruffly.

Taking the folded tissue he pressed into her hand, Susannah wiped her eyes and blew her nose. "I'm not saying guys wouldn't date me, if benefits were involved."

"Now you're really selling yourself short," he told her in a low, gravelly voice.

"But no one wants a ready-made family with five kids."

I would, Gabe thought, much to his surprise. "I'd take you all in a heartbeat," he said before he could stop himself.

Don't miss
His Plan for the Quintuplets *by Cathy Gillen Thacker,*
available July 2020 wherever
Harlequin Special Edition books and ebooks are sold.

Harlequin.com

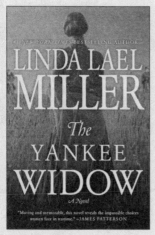